# Lily Graham
## *The*
# CHILD
## OF
# AUSCHWITZ

sphere

SPHERE

First published in 2019 by Bookouture, an imprint of Storyfire Ltd.
This paperback edition published in 2020 by Sphere

1 3 5 7 9 10 8 6 4 2

A CIP catalogue record for this book
is available from the British Library.

ISBN 978-0-7515-7981-9

Printed and bound in Great Britain by
Clays Ltd, Elcograf S.p.A.

Papers used by Sphere are from well-managed forests
and other responsible sources.

MIX
Paper from
responsible sources
FSC® C104740

Sphere
An imprint of
Little, Brown Book Group
Carmelite House
50 Victoria Embankment
London EC4Y 0DZ

An Hachette UK Company

www.hachette.co.uk
www.littlebrown.co.uk

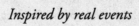

*Inspired by real events*

I was born into a world that had forbidden my existence.

The simple fact of me, had any of the authorities known, would have been enough to end my life before it had even begun.

Still, I came. Small, and half-starved, yet determined to be alive, on one of the coldest nights in one of the darkest places in human history. Not knowing or understanding that my struggle was only just beginning.

The women who helped me bowed their shaved heads and cried the tears I could not as they huddled together with their slight frames to offer me protection.

I barely made a sound, my underdeveloped lungs unable to allow me to cry. It would make my life hard, a price I would pay for all my years, but it is why I survived.

You see, there were children born in Auschwitz.

And I was one of them.

# PRAGUE, PRESENT DAY

It was November and the cold was an uninvited guest. Naděje's knees cracked as she stood up to put another log on the wood burner. Outside, the fog had risen and the streetlight transformed the horizon into an amber, cotton wool haze. It was a muffled, insular sort of night made for reflection, and endless cups of coffee. Bed was a comfort she would deny herself until *it* was done.

She looked at the stack of letters before her, and with her ageing fingers felt the deep scores where her mother's pen had bled rivers of blue.

She'd put this off for too long. Waited for the right moment to tell a story that began long before she was born. For the right words. The right time.

But life doesn't wait till we are ready. More often than not, it throws us into the deep end and asks us to swim. Ready or not.

There was a soft tap on the door, and Kamila, her granddaughter, popped her dark head beyond the door, sighing when she found her at her desk. Her eyes saying a thousand words, with her mouth soon following, as it usually did. 'You'll wear yourself out, *Babička*, keeping this up, you know what the doctor said.'

Naděje peered at the young woman over her glasses, her blue eyes penetrating, the way they did when she was standing at a podium, and asking her students to think about things a different way. 'What do doctors really know about the human spirit, *dítě*? They trust only what they can put in a bottle or explain in black and white. But I have seen what people can do – what they can conquer, what they can *survive* – if they only will it so.'

Kamila knew better than to argue with her grandmother about philosophy. So she tried for a simple, undeniable truth instead. 'But we all need sleep, *Babička*, even you.'

Naděje's lips curled in acknowledgement, and she chose an old lie like a worn pair of slippers, comfortable and familiar. 'Ten more minutes, that's all.' Then she looked up, eyes hopeful. 'And, perhaps, another coffee?'

Kamila made a sound that was a mix of amusement and resignation. 'All right. But after that it's bedtime,' she said firmly, pressing her lips against her grandmother's temple, before making her way to the coffee machine on the other side of the room.

Naděje nodded, but they both knew better. She'd be here till it was done, however long that took. She put her glasses back on her nose, and turned over a fresh sheet of paper. Then she touched the photograph in its gilt frame that was always on her desk, of a young, thin woman with very short dark hair and a baby in her arms.

She had one last story to tell.

Theirs.

And it began in hell on earth.

# ONE

## *Auschwitz, December 1942*

'Are you mad, *Kritzelei*?' hissed Sofie in her ear, eyes huge and full of fear, the criss-cross of scars on her newly shaved head livid against the whiteness of her skull. 'Do you *want* them to shoot us? Keep moving.'

Eva Adami stumbled on beneath a torrent of heavy rain in her too big, mismatched clogs, almost losing one to the thick, relentless mud churned up by thousands of feet before her. It was still dark, perhaps sometime after four a.m. though the harsh floodlights made it appear much later. She hunched over as she moved, trying to keep herself warm. A thankless, futile task. The downpour seemed to bend itself spitefully to slip beneath her neckline. She hated the *Appell*. The twice daily roll call, where they were expected to scramble outside and wait, no matter the weather, no matter whether they were dressed or not, while they were counted and then recounted, for hours and hours on end. Disobedience could cost your life. But then so could almost anything in this place.

She turned to look at her friend, an odd look on her thin face, her hazel-coloured eyes appeared even larger in her head due to her shaved, dark hair. 'We've only been here a week. That's what Helga just said.'

There was a thin exhalation of breath, followed by a low curse. A week. *Here.*

A week since their humanity had been stripped away from them. When they were rounded up like cattle and shoved inside a foul train that stank of death and degradation, barely able to breathe for days with the press of bodies. Only to arrive to utter chaos – noise and shouting, rough handled, then sorted into groups and led into a large hall, where they were stripped and paraded naked in front of leering SS guards, their heads shaved by rough hands. Afterwards they had scrambled to put on clothing, choosing from an array of mismatched used items and spat out.

Eva didn't know that she could still feel shock after all she'd been through so far, but somehow, Helga's words had done it.

'A week in hell,' muttered Vanda, echoing her thoughts. Her red hair, pale skin and freckles belied her Czech-Hungarian heritage. 'It figures that it would feel like an eternity.' She had been on the train with them. They'd travelled standing up for two days. There had been one bucket for food, and one for the shared waste of fifty women.

'You think you need longer than a week to ruin a life?' muttered Helga, sounding disbelieving. She was in her fifties but looked much older, her dark grey hair had begun to grow out in lank strips and her eyes had that glazed look that some of the others had, like she was a walking ghost. She had been here longer than them by several months, and the time had begun to take its toll, especially on her patience with the other new arrivals, like Eva. 'Don't you know by now that a life can flip just like that?' she said, slapping a palm against her thin wrist, causing them all to flinch at the sound like a bullet. She shook her head, then refused to look back at them.

Eva did know. Better than some.

Still, she couldn't help thinking that just a week before, she had no idea that such a place – one designed solely for *extermination* – even existed. A place that made Terezín, the Jewish concentration camp and ghetto outside Prague that she had called home for the past year, seem like a dream.

'No, hell would have been better,' muttered Vanda as Helga moved forward again, and they followed, her lips twitching in a wry semblance of a grin as she looked back at them.

They all turned to look at her, puzzled, as one of the German Shepherds began to snap and snarl on his lead, his fur standing on end, ready to tear them apart, and leave a bloody trail of their remains in the mud.

Vanda gazed back at the dog, not even flinching. 'We'd be warm, at least.'

Eva snorted. It was surprising what one found funny now.

*

At the midday 'meal' they stood in line waiting for their allotted litre of soup. Eva used her hand as a cup for the watery liquid, not getting nearly the amount she was meant to as no matter how hard she tried, without a mug, precious liquid still spilt to the floor. The food had a peculiar smell and taste. There were some who had refused to eat it when they'd first arrived, and even she – who knew far too well about hunger coming from Terezín – had found it hard to choke it down in the beginning, but now they all gulped it desperately. There was a rumour that the guards laced it with something to keep them calm, and to stop their menstruation. It didn't work on the former, and time would tell about the latter. She suspected starvation rations would take care of that eventually anyway, though it wasn't a sure thing, some poor women still got their periods, despite everything.

The soup tasted truly awful, but she would have given anything for more. She had no space in her mind for the fear of what damage possibly poisoned food might do to her body in the long-term, all she could worry about now was surviving today, and that meant trying, somehow, to get more.

In the evenings at around seven, after the workday was complete and they had 'free time' – which they just spent in their barracks anyway – they were given a three-hundred-gram slice of black bread, and a teaspoon of jam or margarine, which they were meant to save half of for breakfast. Few were able to wait, and had to start the day with a grainy coffee substitute that didn't taste of much, until they finally got the soup.

'The first thing we're going to do,' she told Sofie after they'd finished eating, watching as one of the women who'd been here longer stepped forward for a bigger portion, aided by a battered metal mug in her hands, 'is get our own mugs, or maybe even bowls.'

Those with such luxuries managed to get a larger portion as well as bigger pieces of vegetables. Such a simple utensil, but one that could make the difference between life or death here.

Sofie stared, then shook her head, laughing despite herself. The sound was sweet and unexpected, like birdsong on a bleak winter's morning. 'A bowl? Here? *Kritzelei*, always aiming for the stars. And how do you suggest we do that?'

Eva's lips twitched in response, her hazel-coloured eyes alight. Sofie had given her the nickname '*Kritzelei*', back in Terezín where the two had first met. It meant 'doodle', because Eva was prone to daydreaming and seeing the world the way she would like it to be. She had once been an artist and illustrator with a promising future, before the Nazis had decided otherwise.

In Terezín, Eva had become an artist at other things though, through necessity. Like 'sluicing' – redistributing belongings which had been taken away from them in '*The Schleuse*', the area where prisoners were taken in to the camp and dispossessed of their things. Sluicing wasn't really stealing, it was more like giving back, just with interest.

'I don't know yet,' she said watching as a woman, so thin she seemed to have been made of matchsticks, floated past. 'But we have to try. We can't end up like *them*.'

\*

'We call them *Muselmann*,' Helga had whispered, shortly after introducing herself, on their first night in the freezing barracks, where more than a hundred women slept eight to hard, wooden bunks that ran across the room over three levels, resembling cages.

Eva had looked on to where Helga's gnarled, red finger was pointing to a husk-like shape of a woman, whose soul appeared to have checked out some time ago.

'*Muselmann?*'

'Like kneeling men at prayer. All folded in on themselves. They're the ones who have just simply given up.'

Eva blinked, trying to take that in, amongst everything else that had happened today. Was that her future here? Was it Sofie's?

'Can you blame them?' asked Vanda as a young girl, who had also been with them on the train, broke down in sobs.

Suddenly, a *Kapo*, a long-time female prisoner placed in charge of their barracks, came forward and struck the sobbing girl across the face and told her to keep quiet or she'd call a guard to permanently shut her up.

'She's not as cruel as the others,' said Helga, meaning the other *Kapos*, some of whom were as evil as the guards, mimicking their sadism to curry favour with them; some appeared to have retained a semblance of their humanity. As Eva and Sofie stared, Helga explained, 'The crying girl just found out what happened to her mother,' she whispered. 'Better that she learns to just accept it quickly and not make a fuss or she'll follow after her, fast.'

Eva felt a chill run down her spine that had nothing to do with the cold in the freezing barracks. 'Where have they taken her mother?' she asked.

The old woman was hunched over like an old crow, her dusty, greying black hair had begun to grow back, flat and lank against her head, like moth-eaten feathers. She looked at her like the answer was obvious, then pointed outside, even though they couldn't really see out the small cracks. 'To the chimney.'

Eva gasped, clutching onto Sofie as she realised. 'They burn them?'

Sofie closed her eyes in mute horror.

Helga nodded, her expression benign. Her large, dark eyes, rimmed with fine, purplish wrinkles were lifeless, even as she said, 'We're all going to die here. The sooner we accept that the better.' Then she turned around, and lay down, facing the other side of the wall in the bunk, apparently tired of talking, and explaining the inevitable to the new arrivals.

Eva swallowed as she listened to the sound of the girl's muffled sobbing, her heart thudding painfully in her chest. She shared a silent look of horror with Sofie and Vanda.

As night fell they were given a three-inch piece of black bread, and there was nothing to do besides try and sleep. She fitted her body next to Sofie's. The bunk was hard, there was a thin, dirty blanket which they all attempted to share. Despite the press of the others, it was still freezing. Her feet were bare as she hadn't managed to find any socks or stockings after they'd stripped them naked for what passed as a shower, where they had simply smeared water over their dirty skin, and put even dirtier clothes on their cold, wet frames. It would be sometime before they would begin to fear showers, but for now they were blissfully ignorant. For now, processing *this* was enough. She wore a ragamuffin ensemble that consisted of an old, long-sleeved coat dress several sizes too big, and a thin, striped, man's jacket, as well as mismatched clogs, which she was warned to keep on her feet, even as she slept, in case of theft.

She turned over, her eyes staring at the wooden bunk above her head, making them groan as it meant everyone had to turn too. Helga's bleak words reverberated inside her skull, like a sledgehammer.

'We will live,' she whispered to Sofie, reaching for her friend's hand in the dark night. 'We will survive this, like we did Terezín.'

'How?' whispered Sofie.

Her straight-talking, tough-as-anything friend turned dark, fearful eyes towards her. There were heavy shadows beneath her eyes – there had been little sleep on the train and she suspected there would be little sleep in the days ahead too. 'There's a woman here who said they've killed everyone in her village – they were all taken and shot on their first day – almost everyone here has lost their parents or partners, or children.'

Eva stared at her in the dark, trying to take that in.

'Exactly,' hissed Helga, who sat up with a grimace, then turned back to give them a dirty look for keeping her awake. Her eyes were glazed, almost feverish in their sudden anger. A few of the other women moaned at the disturbance. Helga ignored them as she lectured Eva. 'You think you're special? That you, out of everyone here, deserves to live?'

Eva shook her head. 'No. I don't.'

Helga raised a thin brow. 'Yet you think, somehow, you will make it out of this alive?' she hissed.

'Keep quiet!' shouted the *Kapo,* appearing suddenly from her room at the end of the barracks. 'Or I will have you shot here and now!'

They quietened fast.

Eva lay back down, and stared at the wood above her head, then she whispered to Sofie, 'We will live, and I will find Michal again.'

Helga made a sound with the back of her throat, incredulous. 'Your husband?' she guessed. 'You're an absolute *fool*. No one here can afford to think that way – it's better, trust me, to forget who you once were, that life is over now.'

Eva dashed away an angry tear, thinking: *Muselmann*. 'No. *That's* how we can't afford to think – like there's no hope left, because that's the only way they really win.'

# TWO

Auschwitz was the size of a small city. At the entrance to the gates was a lie: *Arbeit Macht Frei*. Work Makes You Free.

Eva flexed her jaw at the thought. Unless the Nazis meant the ultimate freedom –from life. She shuffled forward near a barbed fence in her too-large clogs that slipped and allowed the cold, dirty mud to envelop her frozen toes, causing shooting pains up her calves as she went.

Auschwitz operated as both an extermination and labour camp. It had originally started life as a detention centre for political prisoners, but after Hitler's Final Solution – which called for the mass killing of all Jews, and other non-desirables, such as the disabled, gypsies, homosexuals and others deemed unfit to live in Nazi Germany – it had officially transformed into their largest killing machine.

Eva was in Birkenau, or Auschwitz II-Birkenau as it was officially known, the biggest of the camp facilities, which could hold more than 80,000 prisoners. It was one of over forty such complexes.

Eva looked up past the expanse of mud churned up by tens of thousands of feet, past the long brick building with the guard turret above to the rows of decrepit wooden barracks, to a small team of men a hundred metres away, who were repairing a roof.

Michal was here, somewhere. He could even be amongst *those men*.

She knew that the chances of one of those men being her husband – or even knowing of him, in a camp this size, with so many buildings, covering such vast distances – was slim. But if she could only find a way to speak to them, maybe someone would know something. Maybe someone, somehow, would be able to tell her *something*.

It was why she was here after all.

When everyone in Terezín, which acted as a transit camp as well as ghetto, had tried their best to get their names off the transport lists, Eva had volunteered to come. *Here.* She'd volunteered, hoping to follow her husband, before she'd known exactly what that meant. She wasn't the only wife to do so, countless women were here for the same reason.

An SS guard saw her stare at the group of men, a twitchy hand nearing his gun. She shuffled on in the mud as fast as she could towards the laundry, where she'd been assigned for the day with the other women in the queue up ahead. She raised her chin, and gave one last look at the guard before she went, and thought. *I would do it again. Even knowing what I do now. If it means I find you, Michal. And I will,* she vowed.

\*

It took three days to get the mugs.

She'd used everything her uncle Bedrich had taught her. He'd been a gambler, and trickster, and he'd taught her all he knew back in Terezín, the ghetto, where she along with the rest of her family had been moved after the Nazis occupied Czechoslovakia and they decided that Jewish people were no longer citizens of their own country.

\*

*'Was it this one?' Bedrich asked one night as he picked up the card she'd chosen a minute earlier, which had somehow found itself embedded in his old grey hat.*

*'Yes!' she cried, amazed, her hazel-coloured eyes huge in her heart-shaped face.*

*The laughter lines by his eyes deepened as she gaped at him while he took out the Queen of Spades from the brim. He winked a dark eye, then rolled himself a cigarette.*

*They were in the courtyard, and in the background someone was playing a guitar, a folk song about love and loss. There was even a concert later, with new music by a well-known composer. Sometimes, you could almost convince yourself that this was normal*

18

life, though the poor hygiene, overcrowding, and starvation rations always brought home the truth.

'Hard at work as usual, Bedrich,' said her father; his hazel eyes, so similar to Eva's, were teasing, as he offered a one-fingered salute as he went past. It was a familiar, worn-in joke.

'Always,' was Bedrich's reply, his mouth lifting into a roguish, irrepressible half-grin.

They watched as Eva's father Otto hurried past, a nod for his daughter, and a message that her mother was looking for her.

Her father was a tall, thin man in a suit, with thick grey hair, and kind eyes. His arms were full of paperwork, as he headed towards the camp office, where he worked as a bookkeeper, using his skills as one of the city of Prague's former best accountants to keep the Nazi camp running efficiently.

He wasn't alone, everyone worked here to keep the camp running, whether, like Eva, they worked in the gardens, or her mother who worked in the laundry, or Bedrich who seemed to do all the odd jobs for which you might need a man who didn't ask too many questions. It was all necessary. Few were fortunate enough though to get one of the better jobs like her father. It was due largely to his status of being one of the first arrivals – there was a pecking order, and those who'd helped build the place were at the top as a result. This seemed to imply that they'd had a choice in its construction; they had not. Her father, much to his family's chagrin, failed to utilise the benefit of his status – and more importantly the protection his position may have afforded him.

*Bedrich shook his head and muttered softly, 'Always so busy, Otto, abiding by their rules.'*

*Her uncle caught her staring at him, and pursed his lips, taking a long drag of his rolled cigarette, before pinching it out in his thick fingers and putting the remainder in his grey hat for safekeeping, his black eyes unusually serious.*

*'Eva, listen to me. It's important. Your father is the best man I know, kind, fair. I've looked up to him all my life. Your Babička called me the black sheep of the family, because as you know, I was always getting into trouble. Still do, as a matter-of-fact.' He winked at her at that, his black eyes twinkling, which made her grin; she had always adored her somewhat rapscallion uncle, who always had some get-rich scheme up his sleeve – one of which included, for a time, breeding exotic reptiles, the other was an after-hours poker parlour, the latter did make him quite rich, before it was all taken away.*

*Bedrich continued, 'Your grandmother wanted me to be more like Otto – to have a proper job for life, to see right and wrong in black and white, not shades of grey. Things always need to add up for him. I figure that's why he became an accountant.' He grinned, showing a set of slightly crooked teeth in an infectious smile. He shook his head as he continued. 'He tells me, "Bedrich I'm not going to change who I am, I'm not going to stop standing up for what I believe in, for what is right, and I won't resort to lying and tricks to get ahead in this place. Or cash in on some false sense of entitlement because I was one of the first unlucky people to get here. If my name is on a transport list why must I fight it, if it will just mean someone else must take my place?"'*

*Eva expelled her breath in shock. The lists weren't perfect – or fair, despite what the people who ran them wanted them to believe: all German efficiency, precision and accountability. There were times that you heard of them just randomly adding more people to the transports, which is what they called the trains here. Perfectly healthy people who could work here were torn from their families and sent off 'East' without so much as a goodbye, just to use extra space in a cart, and all because they happened to be in eye line of the guards.*

*It's what had happened to Michal. All she'd known was that he'd been taken, shoved onto a train. Nothing else. Her world had ended in the space of minutes, and the worry and wondering of where they had taken him had been a constant torment ever since. She looked away, eyes clouded with unshed tears.*

*Her uncle pinched the skin between his eyes, nodding, as if he knew exactly what she was thinking. 'I told him, "Otto, don't be a fool, you do it for the same reason you duck when a bullet is fired, you don't have to make it easy for them." But he doesn't listen to me. But maybe you will? I've seen how it is for you – you're small, smaller than the others, always lost in your own little world – sketching, dreaming of a better one with your art, you were always like that, even as a little girl,' he smiled. 'Just like Mila.' They both grew sad thinking of her. His daughter, her cousin and best friend, taken too early from them by scarlet fever,*

21

*which had run rampant in the ghetto in the summer. He looked up, fought back the tears. 'Being sensitive, being small, can be tough in a place like this – you could get walked over if you don't stand your ground. Sometimes that means you have to fight harder to teach others to be fairer, do you understand?'*

*Eva gave a shrug, she knew this already. She had to sometimes use her elbows to ensure that she wasn't forced out of the food line, it was true. If you weren't in line on time you might not get any food, there were no leftovers here. She'd learned that lesson, fast. She hadn't needed a second.*

*He nodded as if he could read her thoughts. 'Sometimes you have to use other skills to survive. Smarts,' he said, tapping his head, and giving her a small wink. 'There are going to be things you do that don't add up out there in the real world. But you must do them anyway. Because we aren't out there, understand? And no one is coming for us anytime soon. There is a different rule book for this place, for this time in our lives. Understand that, and maybe you will get out alive – and I need you to survive this, all right, dítě? We've lost too many already.'*

*Soon afterwards her lessons with her uncle began. They were a welcome distraction from her grief at losing her cousin, and her fears and worries about Michal.*

*She had one goal now, which was to find out where they had taken him – and to follow as soon as she could. But until then, she would learn anything that might help her get out of this alive, and learn she did.*

*Over the course of a week her uncle taught her about sleight of hand, and the art of distraction. In the second week, she could take something off the table without anyone noticing, and in the third, how to put it back without them noticing that either – which, it turned out, was the really tricky bit. She didn't want to steal from her friends or the other residents and she wouldn't, on principle, but she would steal from the guards and her enemies if that's what it took to keep her friends and family alive. She learnt to see that most people don't see what's really going on around them, even when it's happening right beneath their noses. She learnt too that you can help this along with a little distraction if necessary.*

*In three months, she could even do the card trick. It was simple, once you knew how. Like most things really, knowledge was power.*

\*

Getting the mugs had been relatively simple. But it was far from easy. It had taken saving the black rye bread they got for three days to trade with a woman who Helga mentioned could organise such things. A tall, wide-hipped Polish woman named Zuzanna, who handed her three mugs. 'I've organised these for you,' she said, putting one aside. That's what they called it here, 'organising'. Eva eyed the other mug she put to the side.

'I need four,' said Eva, firm.

'That will cost more.'

Eva nodded, offering up a scarf, a prized possession that Sofie had found in the jumble of clothing on arrival, which had been her contribution. Sofie hadn't known that Eva had been starving herself to get the mugs – or she would have given her hell for it. And it had been hell, three days on just fake coffee and watery soup. But food was the biggest ticket item to trade in Auschwitz, with the highest currency.

Zuzanna eyed the ratty but warm, thick scarf then nodded, handing her the fourth mug. The second-highest ticket item was anything that would help with the relentless cold.

It was worth it for a fuller belly – the mugs would ensure that they got at least their share of the soup and coffee, instead of the small handful that trickled through their bare fingers each day. Such a small thing, but it made such a big difference. They were for her, Sofie, Vanda, and another woman, named Noemi, who slept in the bunk below theirs.

She passed Noemi the mug that morning before the *Appell*. Noemi's eyes widened at such a gift. She was a pretty woman, despite her shaved black hair, with pale blue eyes, and high cheekbones.

'For me?' she said, shocked. 'How did you organise this? I owe you, thank you.'

Eva shrugged, giving her a wink. Noemi would owe her, it was just how things were done here, life here existed on a currency of favours – the bigger the favour the bigger the one you *might* get in return; it might come to nothing, or be a little insurance policy for later. All those who were wise did it.

'You're a natural, Eva,' said Vanda as she followed after them, her new mug tight in her hands. She was already speaking of how she would sleep with it tied to her waist, in case of theft, which was also common. People would do anything just to survive.

Eva shrugged, noncommittal. She hadn't been a natural at it in the beginning, not by a long shot, far too prone to daydreaming and far too soft-hearted. But Bedrich had taught her well.

# THREE

Snow was beginning to fall in thick drifts that swirled around the women as they moved forward, fighting coughs or sneezes. Those who were shrewd made themselves appear stronger, fitter, able to work. Those who didn't were at risk of getting the sort of jobs that ensured their quick demise.

The noise coming from the vast lines of women, even with the muffling effects of the snow, was loud like the drone of bees. Eva stood on numbed toes, back straight so that she could appear taller, and stronger. Stockings would be her next order of business, she decided. In the back of her mind she was beginning to really worry about frostbite.

But it was nothing compared to Vanda's current problem. The Hungarian swallowed, her wide lips tight in her face, where her pale freckled skin had lost all its colour, making her shorn ginger hair glow in the weak winter light.

An SS guard by the name of Wilhem Hinterschloss – cold grey eyes, thin lips, and even thinner, spindle-like teeth – was glaring at her as if she were an insect he'd like to squash, and soon.

He repeated his instruction, his jaw flexing as he did, but it was clear that Vanda, whose German was limited at best, still didn't understand.

'The warehouse,' Eva whispered, shuffling closer, heart thudding in fear. 'They want you to go to the sorting warehouse, the one they call "Kanada".'

Nicknamed so by the inmates after a place they deemed as a land of plenty, it was spelt with a 'K' in German.

Hinterschloss turned sharply towards her, grey eyes flaring – the whites were yellow, like they had been dipped in nicotine. His voice was cold and low, and it cut into her deeper than the icy weather. 'What did you just say?'

A chill ran down Eva's spine, and her mouth turned suddenly dry.

There was a flash of the rat-like teeth, and Eva was reminded strongly of a rodent about to feast on its prey.

Eva's heart began to thud, her arms and legs turned suddenly numb. Her tongue was too large for her mouth as she attempted to formulate a response.

She swallowed as he stepped forward, his thick, hobnailed boots sinking into the snow, his face inches from hers. He smelt of stale breath and whisky. It figured the guards used something to numb the cold while they waited outside with them; they didn't seem to need it for their hearts. They didn't have any.

Eva hesitated. 'I-I was translating, sir.'

Hinterschloss's hands drifted towards his gun and Eva closed her eyes for a moment in abject fear. The first time she met Sofie, in the Jewish ghetto, before she'd begun her 'lessons' with her uncle, raced before her mind, suddenly, unbidden.

\*

*'You speak German?'*

*Eva looked up from her sketchbook. It was just a collection of torn scraps of paper that she'd assembled into a book with twine that she'd traded a potato for. The woman who had been moved into their barracks that morning was standing by her bunk. She had yet to find a bed. Space was always an issue, here. She was tall and thin, wearing an old green dress that was fraying at the edges. She had long, dark blonde hair, and big dark eyes. At the top of her forehead, running into her hairline, was a thick, knotty wound that had started to scab — it looked like it would become a rather large scar. In spite of this, or perhaps in contrast to the scar, Eva couldn't help noticing that she was very pretty, with full lips and sharp cheekbones.*

*In the background, Eva tuned in to two women having an argument that she hadn't been aware of while she sketched. The rationed food and close confinement, combined with the constant threat of being transported to a labour camp away from their families, made for a tense environment. Eva often opted out of it all by retreating to the past, with her sketches.*

28

She looked up at the stranger's large, dark, curious eyes as she took a seat beside her. Then she shrugged, answering her question. 'Not really. Everyone here speaks Czech.'

'That's mad.'

Eva's long, dark hair swung forward as she stared at the new girl in surprise. 'Why mad?'

'The inmates speak it, Kritzelei, but the people in charge, the people making the rules, who you might have to get things out of – they speak German.'

Eva's hazel eyes widened in disbelief at the strange girl's words, and even stranger ideas. 'Get things out of the Germans?' she repeated, 'Like what, a bullet?' She shook her head, and turned back to her drawing of the Vltava river, just after spring, when the kingcups were in bloom. It was where she wished she was, more than anywhere else. Back home. She carried on speaking as she sketched, 'Don't you see, they'll never see us as one of them, that's why we're here.'

It was a simple fact. It was why they'd been rounded up and taken from their homes, and forced to live in this hellish Jewish ghetto.

'Yes, they will never think of you as one of them, but you can give them one less reason to treat you like an animal. By knowing their language.'

Eva frowned as she considered. That made sense, and it might help her if she was ever to find where they had taken her husband. She looked up, lifting the pencil.

'How though?'

'I'll teach you.'

'Why? Why would you do that?'

'Because,' she grinned. 'I have heard that you have room in your bunk – is that true?'

'Yes.'

It had recently come available, as the woman she'd been sharing it with had been moved on – transported out to another camp, somewhere 'East' like the others, who knew where?

The woman leant forward from her seat by the edge of the bed. 'So, it's for me then, right?' Then she grinned, and it transformed her face, made her young and impish, instantly likable. 'I'm Sofie Weis, by the way.'

Eva stared at her, and she grinned in return. 'All right,' she agreed, and introduced herself too. 'Eva Adami.'

Sofie was a hard task master. She was tough, and straight-talking, and tolerated no arguments, especially when it came to Eva's pronunciation, and as the weeks passed she ruled with an iron fist.

'No, Kritzelei. Flatten your lips, don't round things out so.'

'What does it matter?' sighed Eva. She despised everything about the Germans, she couldn't help it – look what they'd done to them, how they forced them to live, it galled her to learn it, to try sounding just like them. 'So, I'll have an accent, and won't sound like them, so what?'

Sofie shook her head, exasperated. 'Think, Kritzelei, and then they kill you because you sound different.'

30

Eva rolled her eyes. 'They wouldn't kill me just for that.'

Sofie laughed, and pushed back a long strand of dark blonde hair from her face. Eva's eye fell on the thick wound on her forehead and scalp that had turned into a large pink scar. It was an involuntary movement, that had nonetheless proved Sofie's point more than she realised. 'What must it be like living in that head of yours?' muttered Sofie. 'All rainbows and fair play…'

Eva clenched her jaw. She wasn't an idiot, she just chose not to focus on how bad everything was all the time. She'd made it here so far, hadn't she? She'd managed to keep her name off a transport list, to eat, to survive. To do everything in her power to try find out where they'd taken Michal.

'I'm not a fool, you don't need to mock me just because I choose not to spend all my time here beating my head against the wall, because I have hope that someday I'll get out of here.'

Sofie's eyes softened, she looked sad. 'I'm not mocking you. I admire it, honestly. I like your version of the world much better,' she said, pointing to the wall by their bunk, where Eva's sketches were tacked on, offering an escape from the grim surrounds. There were drawings of Eva's beloved city, the Vltava river, and the Prague Castle. A touch of home.

'But in the Westerbork camp that I was taken to, I met others who hadn't been treated so kindly – who'd come from much harsher places. Where there were no concerts or friends or families getting to see one another – or bathrooms with showers and toilets. Where they were treated like scum, and could be killed just for being in the wrong place. I was meant to go to one of these places further east,' she said, her eyes growing darker. 'The only reason they took me here to Terezín instead, was because the train taking us broke down and in the mix-up, I joined the one coming here. Just pure luck that I chose it. I want you to be aware of that, and to be safe. You know the plan is to send everyone out of here to one of those places where we will work outside or in a factory for hours. So, I need you to be prepared, okay? At the station, I saw them kill a man just because he tripped and got in the guard's way. Rather than move him, they shot him in case he did it again.'

Eva blinked, trying to take that in. That there were places where life had become so worthless that it could be scrubbed out just for getting in someone's way, like an insect.

'But if they hate us that much, why try to be more like them, why bother trying to sound like them?'

Sofie shrugged. 'Because the smallest thing here can make a big difference. Which line you're in, what train you end up on. The fly that sees that the window is open by a crack lives, Kritzelei. The one that doesn't just beats itself to death against the glass.'

*

'Translating?' Hinterschloss repeated, his grey eyes turning to slits in his ruddy face. 'Do you think I need translating? Do we have time to waste, scum?' He spat, and the spittle froze before it hit her feet.

Eva shook her head, quickly. 'No, you do not. That is why I wanted to help – so that the people you told to go work in the warehouse understood your instruction.'

He stared at her for a moment, 'You wanted to help?' he repeated, softly. His hand fluttered back to his pistol. He sniffed, then made a barely imperceptible nod of his head as if he were considering which course of action to take. It was freezing, they'd been outside for more than two hours already. Perhaps, he too was feeling that, or the effects of the whisky were wearing thin, because, at last, he sighed and said, 'Fine, go with them then, make sure they understand where to go and what to do.'

Eva blew out her breath. Her knees were so shaky, if she moved she'd fall over. All she could do was nod with abject relief.

'You either have a death wish,' Vanda told her as they began the long walk through the snow to the warehouses, Eva's heart still thundering loudly in her ears, 'or the biggest balls I have ever seen,' she laughed. A few of the others joined in.

Sofie huffed behind her; she and Helga had also been assigned to the warehouse, her eyes wide, serious. 'Don't be an idiot, she just saved your life.'

It was still cold, the kind that seemed to bite. They'd moved to a new barrack with the others assigned to the warehouse, which was a slight improvement on the previous, mainly at present, due to an extra ratty blanket they could share. Not that it helped much. The wind had picked up, making a howling noise that shook the rafters, and caused them all to shiver, miserably. In one of the other bunks a woman was loudly coughing, keeping everyone awake. 'Your elbow is digging into me,' complained Sofie, and Eva shifted over again.

Clearly uncomfortable, and unable to sleep, Sofie sighed, ran a hand over her shorn, scarred head, and said, 'Tell me again, about the river, about the *sun*. About the day you met Michal.'

Eva looked up, a small smile butterflying across her lips, and she shuffled closer to lean her shaved head against Sofie's bony shoulder.

There were other voices from the bunk, who echoed hers, asking the same. 'Yes, tell us, *Kritzelei*, about the boy, and when you met.'

'And the peach, don't forget to describe the peach,' said Helga, who had warmed to her over time. Perhaps some of Eva's natural hopeful nature had rubbed off just a little on the old woman, who wasn't nearly as sharp as she had been when they'd first met; the pair had become something of unlikely friends.

The other bunkmates groaned, their stomachs rumbling in their hunger, mouths salivating at the thought of the ripe, sun-warmed peach, with its golden flesh and sweet juice.

Eva smiled in the dark night, she'd told them the story already, but she didn't mind telling it again. That's what she did most nights, tell stories. She used to draw pictures with her fingers, now she just did it with her words, and her memories. It wasn't that different in the end.

'It was 1938, and early April in Prague. Spring had arrived early that year, making up for the long winter. It was that rare sort of day, when the wind is cool, but not cold, and you start to dream that summer might just be on its way. The kingcups were in bloom, and you could smell them on the banks of the river. The old town was busy, people were going to the market, and I was sitting by a fountain.

'I'd got out of the house early, trying to distract myself from the news – all we did at home was worry about what was happening with Germany since they had annexed Austria. Hitler had declared that he was looking at Czechoslovakia next, but we had faith that President Beneš would never allow it, or the allies for that matter, or at least, we were trying to keep the faith…'

'Which was when you saw the most beautiful—' interrupted Vanda, her short red hair bright even in the dark barracks.

'No, when she heard the most beautiful music,' corrected Sofie, narrowing her dark eyes at her. 'And stop interrupting the story, I was just starting to feel the sun on my fingers.'

She held up her poor, red hands which were swollen and sore from the cold. Frostbite was a real problem in the camp, along with everything else.

Eva took them and cupped them between her own.

'That's right,' she continued. 'I was sitting by the fountain with my sketchbook, the sunshine was pooling down, and it was warm, out of the wind. In front of me was a peach that I was trying to draw, except my mind kept getting dragged back to my father's worried eyes, to the fear that we would perhaps enter another war. I was wondering if I should just go for a walk instead, leave my gloomy thoughts behind, when I heard the most beautiful music. A violin began to play and I felt as if maybe I'd stumbled into a dream. It was soft at first, then haunting. The melody seemed to carry me away, and I must have sat for ten minutes just listening. I couldn't see where it was coming from, so I got up to walk around and look. But there was no one. Then finally, I glanced up, and I saw that I was sitting directly beneath a studio and above me was a man playing. All I could see from my position were his shoes.'

'You couldn't see his face at all?' asked Vanda.

'No.'

'Were they nice shoes?' asked Helga.

'They were old.'

'Still, you decided to give him your peach?'

They all laughed.

So did Eva. 'Yes, when I was finished drawing I left it on the windowsill, it was the only part I could reach.'

'Why did you do that?' asked Vanda.

Eva shrugged. 'I don't know. I wanted to give him something in return, something for what he'd just given me.'

36

'What was that?'

'Hope.'

Eva had come back to the square the next day, and smiled when she saw that the peach was no longer there. That maybe he had taken it.

'It might have been carried away by a cat or a bird,' said Helga, ever practical.

'Maybe,' Eva acknowledged.

Still, she waited by the fountain, with her sketchbook, and another peach.

It was some time before the music began again.

As Eva sat and listened, she closed her eyes. The weather had turned cold again, a typical fickle spring, but she was content just to sit and savour the music, wrapped beneath a thick scarlet shawl. Her long dark hair beneath a cream woollen hat. The melody was haunting, and beautiful, and it seemed to touch her very soul.

'And still you never saw his face?'

Eva shook her head. 'Just the shoes – and the rug, it was navy and bottle green, which he stepped on as he played. It was threadbare in the places where he moved.'

She came back every day after that to listen to him play. To sketch, whatever the weather. Each day when she turned to leave, she left him an offering. A peach. An apple. Once, a square of chocolate.

It was this that caused them all to groan now. 'Imagine if he'd never taken it. The waste!' one of the women cried.

No one wasted food here. They all nodded.

Then one day, she came back to the square, to take her seat by the fountain, and she saw that he'd left her something by the windowsill. It was a note, 'For the peach-girl,' it read.

'And what was it?' asked Helga.

'Tickets to the symphony that night.'

'Did you know he played in the symphony?'

'Not until then, no. I didn't have a dress that was suitable. So I borrowed one from my cousin, Mila, a blue dress. She was something of a socialite.' She smiled at the memory of her favourite cousin, whom she missed terribly. 'Silk.'

Eva shook her head at the memory. It had been so taken for granted. Fine clothes. Being clean. It was a world away from the scratchy, dirty rags they all wore now, each with some form of the striped uniforms that made them all look the same, like yet another number.

'Who did you take?' asked Sofie. Even though she knew the story now, by heart.

Eva grinned. 'I took my mother.'

'On a date!' laughed Vanda. She had a deep, naughty, back-of-the-classroom sort of laugh that made them all chortle too.

'I didn't know it was a date! I was just going to the symphony.'

'But you didn't know which one he was? How romantic,' she cried, her eyes dancing at the thought.

'Though he could have been ugly and fat,' argued Helga.

The others all rolled their eyes at her, but Eva acknowledged this with a shrug. 'No, she's right, he could have been anyone, well, anyone in the violin section at least.'

'Did you think maybe you'd recognise him somehow – like if he played a solo?' asked Vanda, as the wind picked up outside, creating a howling noise that swept through the barracks and made them all huddle closer together.

Eva played with the worn fabric on her wrist, her mind in the past, not feeling the cold, for once. Even now if she closed her eyes she could hear the violins, keeping time to the beat of her heart.

'I hoped that was the case. But as soon as the evening's performance began I realised that he couldn't be the lead violinist – I'd only find out much later that it will take an act of divine intervention to become a soloist – it's really hard, especially when you are young. But I didn't know he was young, yet.' She smiled.

'How did you know he wasn't a soloist?'

Eva's eyes shone as she remembered. 'Well, it was the music, he didn't play like I'd heard. It was faster, precise, but the emotion wasn't the same. So, I closed my eyes, and then, somehow, I heard him there in the front. When I opened my eyes, I found him. I remember grabbing my mother's hand.'

'How – how did you know it was him?'

She grinned. 'I recognised the shoes.'

# FOUR

Eva's intervention on Vanda's behalf had been the first bit of real good fortune she'd had since she'd arrived.

The set of warehouses known as 'Kanada' went on for what seemed like miles.

It was the land of plenty, and easily the most prized work assignment in the camp. It was where they stored the belongings that had been taken from all the prisoners when they'd arrived, all of which needed to be sorted and classified. These items – from the perambulators of Jewish mothers to the dentures of Jewish men – would be utilised by the German population. *Waste not, want not.*

She wondered if they even knew where the government's supply came from, or if they cared at all. Seeing the vast number of things that had been taken from them, and realising that most of these people were probably now dead, was a horrifying thought.

Eva's task was to go through the men's coats and to search the lining for valuables; anything that could be potentially useful for those unnamed German people.

Theft was punishable by death. If you were caught.

Eva had learnt how to hide things well, from two years' worth years of 'sluicing' in Terezín. Like how to unpick the stitches in a sleeve if it was lined, the perfect place to hide something small, like a slip of paper, or a flat watch. Collars could hold jewels, if you were lucky enough to find them, which could be traded for extra food or information. In the knees of stockings was a good place for hiding extra potatoes she dug up when she worked in the gardens of Terezín. Softer fruit like bananas, and vegetables like cucumbers, made excellent hideaways in brassieres. She'd taken things that could stand a bit of jostle and wear – tomatoes, not so much. She didn't know if there were gardens here, somehow she doubted it.

In the vast piles of men's coats she found money, and jewels, and sometimes bits of dried food, which could be useful for trading and bartering. She used this to finally get some new clogs – both the same size to fit her small feet, as well as several thick and scratchy pairs of socks, two sets of stockings and two long and thick woollen scarves. One for her and one for Sofie.

She was so quick that no one ever saw her do it, despite the fact that the guards patrolled regularly. The advantage of the warehouse being so enormous was that there were plenty of opportunities when the guards moved on for even the slowest of the bunch to take something, and they all did, despite the risks. Still, few were as good as Eva. She only took things she knew she could hide, and hide well.

\*

*'If you're going to steal, you've got to face the very real possibility that you will get caught,' her uncle Bedrich had warned her, his dark eyes serious, when he'd turned to find her trying and failing to take his watch off him. He bent her arm back, playfully, but it still hurt. She winced, rubbing her arm.*

*'That hurt! You told me to try it!'*

*He laughed, ignoring her protests. 'No, dítě, getting your head blown off will* hurt.*' He held up something in his other hand, eyes dancing.*

*It was her tiny stub of a pencil, with the bite marks at the end. She blinked, then touched her coat. How had he got it without her even feeling it? He waggled a gnarled finger at her and said, 'Try better. Try harder. Only steal if you are absolutely sure it's worth it.'*

*She'd raised a brow, looking at her pencil which he pocketed with a grin to her deep annoyance. It was her last one, and was, as such, rather valuable. 'And was it – taking that from me?'*

*'To teach my favourite niece this lesson, I'd say it was.' Then he sauntered off, turning back to add, 'Very,' with a chuckle, and he left whistling a tune as he went. She'd shaken her head as she watched him go, a reluctant smile on her lips. Without looking back, he doffed his grey hat to her, and was gone with the night.*

*It took her three more attempts but eventually she got the pencil back from him. And his watch.*

\*

She looked up now as Hinterschloss walked past, her hand making a quick splaying action so that the crinkled package sped up her sleeve, fast. He stopped and looked at her, and she shook out the coat, and placed it on top of the others. He moved on, oblivious to the slim parcel sliding up her sleeve, which would be squirrelled away, and placed in the stockings by her knees in a minute.

Sofie, who had also been transferred to the Kanada work unit was put in another part of the building, sorting through bedding, a welcome relief from her old posting in laundry – brutal work, especially on her back and fingers, the skin of which had begun to itch and split from the harsh soap, making it all the more painful in the cold. But it was harder for her to sneak anything away, like the others, as a young guard named Fritz Meier, with a round, slightly effeminate face with big blue eyes, plump lips and sandy blond hair always seemed to find some reason to be where she was.

'Chocolate, *Kritzelei*,' sighed Sofie as she put a small piece on her tongue later that evening.

Eva nodded, eyes alight, as she shared it with the others in her bunk; it was the first time in weeks that she felt even slightly normal. It had grown white with age, but it still tasted heavenly.

'I didn't think I'd ever taste chocolate again,' said Helga, sucking it, a look of pure bliss on her old face. 'We're lucky to have been assigned here,' said Eva, chewing her own sliver of chocolate slowly, her eyes closed in pleasure.

Helga looked at them, her eyes softer than they usually were, and full of warning. 'If we were wise, we'd try to get an assignment away from the warehouses as quick as we can – I've heard that not many come back after they've been sent here.'

'What do you mean?' asked Sofie, turning to look at her in surprise.

'Well, when you finish for the day, it's quicker to walk you to the crematoria and dispose of you there than take you back here to the barracks.'

At her frown, the old woman explained. 'They're there behind the warehouse – the gas chambers and crematoria – they've been working them day and night, that's what Sara said,' she whispered, her eye darting to their new *Kapo*, at the end of their barracks who was busy cooking her evening meal, one she wouldn't be sharing.

The stolen chocolate stuck in Eva's throat.

What Eva found more often than not in the linings and pockets of the coats and jackets she sorted weren't jewels or money, but the photographs of loved ones. When people were unsure of what to take, or if they would ever see their friends or family again, what they prized more than gold or jewels were the faces of the people that they loved.

It was these that Eva would treat with the most respect, piling them up in a corner, and stacking them together. Her eyes were drawn to the children, to the mothers, the sons and daughters, to the lovers. Snapped in time, all these memories, all these *lives*, snatched away.

'They will make you burn these, or at least turn them over,' said another woman who had been assigned the same task, seeing Eva put another photograph on a pile. 'I doubt even they want to be reminded of what they've done – to see that these were people once,' she said, nodding at the pile of coats. Then she picked up the stack of photographs Eva had been sorting and took them away herself.

Eva's fist clenched. 'Before they turned us into rats, into animals, fighting for crumbs, you mean?' She had to stop herself from protesting as the woman took the photographs to the guard, where Eva was sure they would be destroyed.

She stared at the back of the woman's head, feeling oddly betrayed. Eva returned to her work, and saw that one of the photographs had fallen on the floor, and she stooped to pick it up. It was instinctive. It was a picture of a family, a man with bushy eyebrows and a mole over his lips. He had his arms around a shy girl who could barely meet the camera's gaze, and a boy who was in front laughing. She touched it, and her lips moved in the ghost of a smile. They could have just posed for this picture now. Without really knowing why, Eva slipped it up her sleeve.

She wouldn't forget that they were human. That they were people once, who had lived lives full of joy and heartbreak.

They had had jobs, and mortgages and homes filled with families and food and love. She wouldn't forget, either, that she had been a person once, too, with a life, a future, a family, and a home, like them.

# FIVE

Working in the Kanada was one of the easiest roles in the camp. The hours were long, yes, but the work itself was easy and the rewards, if you had nimble fingers, like Eva, were great. Sofie was pretty good at sluicing the odd item here and there, despite the fact that they were regularly searched; shoes were good hiding spots that weren't really checked. She'd got lucky with a bracelet the week before, and had managed to trade it with the women who worked in the kitchens for salami and cheese, and it had been wonderful to have a full belly for the first time in months. She'd given some of the cheese to their *Kapo*. As a result, Sofie and Eva were able to use the washrooms for the first time in ages, which was wonderful, not that they were perfectly clean but less dirty was better than the alternative.

But it was getting harder for her to steal anything much, as her work was closely supervised by the guard, Meier. His big blue eyes were often cast towards her, and his innocent-looking face had the kind of boyish, worrisome flush to his cheeks whenever she looked in his direction, that let her know he would cause trouble.

Sofie could feel his eyes on her now. She looked up and saw him smile at her. She looked down, with a frown, gritting her teeth. An older woman that had been assigned the same task as her snorted, then whispered loudly, so he could hear.

'Looks like someone's in love.'

Sofie looked up to see that Meier's ears had turned red in embarrassment, and he looked away.

The old woman started to laugh as his blush deepened.

Sofie felt her heart thud in fear. The woman was an idiot. He might be young and barely out of puberty but it would be a mistake to antagonise someone like him. 'Shut up,' she snapped at the old woman. 'No one asked you.'

The other guard, Hinterschloss, came in and told them to keep it down.

Sofie flexed her jaw and carried on working, when she glanced up sometime later she saw Meier look at her, a soft expression on his face. She looked away again, wondering if she'd just encouraged him more, cursing herself in the process.

As they walked, she told Eva about her fears. '*Kritzelei*, he follows me everywhere. This is the only time he doesn't, when we go to the latrine.'

Eva frowned. 'I don't think you have anything to worry about, I think he's basically harmless.'

'For now,' agreed Sofie.

'At least it's not Hinterschloss,' said Eva. The foul-tempered guard seemed to reserve his antics for their side of the building. Like calling them names, and telling them if they didn't find him anything good he would make them skip their midday meal. Just the day before he'd kicked one of the women to the ground for walking too slowly on the way out of the warehouse – though he'd been known to do the same if they rushed, sneering, 'In such a hurry to die, eh?' He'd hit them on the backs of the legs with the butt of his rifle. 'I'm not sure he's capable of any emotion besides spite,' said Eva.

Sofie nodded. It could be worse.

When she got back to her work though, and found a note with the words, 'I missed you,' scribbled on a tiny slip of paper near where she'd been sorting through blankets, and saw Meier shooting her surreptitious looks from his post by the wall, she knew that actually, worse might be on its way.

*

'You're pretty, you know that?' he said later, coming to stand near her, on the pretext of helping her fold a blanket. He peered at her slim body in approval.

Sofie closed her eyes but tried to keep her expression light. Ordinarily she would tell someone like him to get lost, with some choice words so that he never attempted it again. She was direct, and people often mistook it as rudeness. But she had learnt, like Eva, that there were some games you had to play in order to survive.

'Not with this,' she said, running a hand over the scar along her forehead and scalp, where her dark blonde hair was starting to grow back.

'How did you get it?' he asked, his eyes concerned.

Sofie felt her anger rise at the question. The windows of her father's watchmaking shop exploding in a sea of glass, her son's loud wails, her blood pooling on the floor, all flashed before her eyes. She wanted to snap, 'How do you think?' To hiss in his face, that it was from boys like him. Instead she took a breath and lied. 'I fell down some stairs.'

'Oh. Well, you're still pretty.'

Sofie didn't say anything.

'We watched a film in the cinema last night – starring Bette Davis, and I couldn't help thinking that you look just like her, prettier even, because you don't wear any make-up.'

Sofie looked up at him, noting his clear blue eyes. 'The cinema?'

'Oh yes, there's lots to do in this town.'

He didn't seem to notice the look of incredulity she shot him.

That night as they lay in their bunk and the snow fell in thick drifts outside, they shivered, huddling together, Sofie asked, 'Did you know that there's a cinema here?'

'A cinema?' said Eva turning to look at her in surprise, eyes wide in disbelief.

'For the guards.'

'I suppose they need something to do with their evenings,' scoffed Vanda, sarcastically.

'Still, while we're here suffering, dying, they're watching films.'

It was a disturbing thought.

*

As the others fell asleep, Sofie stared at the wood from the bunk bed above, thinking of those guards at the cinema, calling this place a 'town' while for them it was a prison. The sensible thing to do, she knew, was to use Meier and his infatuation with her to get what she needed out of him. Eva wasn't the only person who had come to Auschwitz looking for someone. Only, unlike her friend, it wasn't a happy reunion she was after.

# SIX

There were always new transports arriving. Every day thousands more women arrived in Auschwitz, their fate decided as they lined up in groups: left or right.

Word spread like wildfire of where they were from – camps like Westerbork, Terezín, Ravensbruck – and Eva and Sofie would rush to meet the new arrivals, with the others, particularly if they were from anywhere they had been themselves.

After the evening *Appell*, you sometimes found cousins reunited, friends, or even mothers and daughters, though it was usually more distant connections one came across: strangers with whom you'd shared passing greetings, light conversations about the weather back home, your family's good health. People you never thought you'd see reduced to the bare bones of who they used to be.

There was Mrs Edelstein the greengrocer from Eva's street, who used to always add something extra in a bag when she was out shopping with her mother. 'Take, take,' she used to say, offering her a handful of sugared almonds, or a ripe nectarine. Always with a ready smile for her. Seeing the poor woman here, with her shocked face and shaved hair, had been heartbreaking. She had been in Terezín up until now, though Eva hadn't seen her there.

'Have you any news about my parents?' Eva asked.

She shook her head. 'No, I didn't see them, I'm sorry, we left so suddenly, they took my sons from me,' her lips started to tremble, 'I don't know if they'll live,' and then she began to cry.

Eva rushed forward and the two hugged for a long time. Strangers no more.


She wasn't the only one who encountered people she used to know. Every evening before curfew, Sofie made the rounds, asking the women if they knew where she could find her cousin. 'Her name is Lotte,' she told them. 'I need to find her. They said she was brought here. She would have been taken to the Austrian barracks, I think.'

Sofie passed around some extra bread she'd traded for. 'She has blonde hair, big green eyes.'

But no one had heard anything. 'Sometimes people go by another name here,' one of the others suggested. 'A nickname, or something else, is there anything else you can think of?' she said, pocketing the bread.

Sofie sniffed. 'Yes.' It wasn't a nickname though. It was what she would call her if she ever found her again.

'What?'

'*Brutus*. Or perhaps Judas,' she said with a snort, aware of the irony.

# SEVEN

Sofie's palm closed over the ring. She'd found it in the lining of the bedding she was looking through in the warehouse. Her gaze had darted left and right nervously, and she'd seen no one looking. She slipped it up her sleeve.

There was a shuffling sound behind her, and she froze, a prickle of fear ripping through her. 'Open your hand,' said a soft voice, close to her ear. Sofie lifted her gaze, just over her shoulder. Meier. His blue gaze was oddly still, serious. She swallowed. 'Open it,' he said, more firmly.

Sofie obeyed. She bit her lip. 'I-I was going to bring this to you.'

He looked at her for a long moment, his gaze gave nothing away. For a moment, Sofie was wrenched back in the past, to a moment just like this, when she'd thought that her life might be over. Except then she'd had Eva come to her rescue.

*

*'Let her go.' Eva raced at the gendarme, a tangle of limbs and flying dark hair, as she tried to pull Sofie out of the gendarme's grip.*

'Don't, Kritzelei,' Sofie implored as the guard pushed her back roughly, so that she landed roughly on her backside in the muddy courtyard. He was tall, with short, dark hair and hooded eyes, which peered at Eva in some surprise. 'This does not concern you, girl – I suggest for your sake that you move on.'

Then he twisted Sofie's arm, and attempted to drag her off to the camp office, while she resisted. Eva could see that her friend's arm had turned white, and bloodless, like her face which was pale, and terrified. The scar on her forehead stood out in sharp pink relief.

'What has she done?' demanded Eva, dusting herself off and getting back up, ready to implore, to beg. The gendarmes in Terezín were generally reasonable, and could be persuaded, or bribed, so she'd found. 'Maybe I can help?'

The gendarme looked at her, his eyes dark, as he prised open Sofie's fingers, while she tried desperately to keep her fist closed. 'She has been found sending illegal letters, the punishment – as all of you know – is death.'

Correspondence with the outside was strictly controlled – in the beginning no one in the ghetto was allowed to send any. In January of 1942, a few prisoners were caught, and the gendarmes had made an example of them, with an horrific public execution that had rocked the camp, and truly driven home to them just where they were. A prison.

Inmates could send out short postcards, written in German, that were censored. At one time these were limited to a strict word count but that had since been abolished. Still, it was almost impossible to say anything of importance in the postcards or find out anything of importance either. Keeping the illusion that Terezín was a 'model' camp with happy inmates, and no suffering was vital to the Nazis as it had come under a lot of scrutiny. In fact, there would even be an inspection to this effect by the Red Cross many months from now.

'Illegal letters?' said Eva. 'I'm sure that's not true. The only ones she sends are the postcards. You must have some kind of proof – even here, there needs to be proof for such an accusation?'

Sofie's eyes widened, wondering at what game her friend was playing. The gendarme looked at Eva as if she was an idiot. 'Of course, there is proof!' Then he took Eva's hand roughly and prised open her fingers, in triumph. Only to blink. In Sofie's splayed fingers was no letter, just a small crumpled up bill of no real significance. It was the currency used here, 'ghettogeld' they called it.

He stared at in shock. Then shook Sofie roughly. 'It was there, I saw it!'

'I -I -I was just going to buy some bread,' stammered Sofie.

'You're lying!' he hissed.

Eva frowned. 'Maybe you saw this and thought it was a letter – perhaps it looks like it from far.'

Sofie nodded, emphatically.

The gendarme looked livid. 'I know what I saw! She's hidden it. But I will find it.' And he began searching Sofie's body, patting her down, making her turn out her pockets, take off her shoes.

He even squeezed open her mouth to see if she'd tried to swallow it, but found nothing.

Suddenly he straightened – something must have occurred to him – whirling around to look at her suspiciously. 'You touched her earlier – I saw it, when you rushed at her. You took it, didn't you?'

Eva's eyes widened. 'You were holding on to her arm the whole time – and you found it there in her hand. I'm no magician.'

He swore, then told her to hold out her arms while he began searching her too.

Eva's eyes were calm even as his hands swept over her undergarments. Finding nothing, he looked furious, gritting his teeth, and pushing her from him, towards Sofie.

'Maybe you should get your eyes tested?' suggested Eva sweetly.

His arm circled back and he hooked her with his left fist – she went flying into the ground. He spat, 'I know what I saw, you won't get so lucky next time.'

There was blood on the ground, and Eva's nose was broken. Her left eye would be swollen shut for days. Sofie helped her back to their barracks and attempted to mop up her face. As she applied ointment that she'd got from one of the other women in the barracks to her friend's eye, Sofie shook her head and asked, 'How did you do it? Do you have a death wish, Kritzelei?'

'Do you?' retorted Eva, spitting out blood into a nearby bowl. 'No.'

Sofie shook her head, and dabbed some more ointment on Eva's eyelid, making her flinch.

*Then she sighed, again. 'Tell me how you did it.'*

*'Did what?'*

*Sofie shook her head. 'You know what I mean, the letter?'*

*Eva gave her a lopsided grin and then made something appear from behind her friend's ear. 'You mean this letter?'*

*Sofie gasped, then made to grab it.*

*Eva made the letter disappear just as fast as it appeared. Like magic.*

*'Kritzelei!' protested Sofie. 'I still need to send that letter.'*

*'I know you do – but that gendarme has it in for you – and trust me you'll get caught.'*

*'And you won't?'*

*'Do I ever?'*

*Sofie crossed her arms. She appreciated what her friend had done for her, more than she could say, but she didn't want her to risk her life for her.*

*'Eva, that gendarme is going to have it in for you too – I saw the way he looked at you.'*

*'Don't worry about it – I'll think of something.'*

*When Bedrich saw Eva's face, he tutted. 'I heard about what happened. You risked your life for this girl. Why?'*

*'She's my friend, uncle.'*

*'So?'*

*'So that means something to me.'*

*Bedrich sniffed. 'What if you'd got caught, Eva? It's a serious offence – you know that – you might not survive if they catch you.'*

*Eva grinned, then bit off a small wedge of salami. Then she handed it to him. He frowned, touched his jacket pocket from where she'd taken it without him noticing, and then snorted, giving her his half smile, as he ruffled her hair in a one arm hug.*

*'They'll have to try,' she said.*

*Two weeks later, she was able to send out Sofie's letter. She arranged it through one of the work units who went out to the fields – they passed by the outside world, many having made a few connections with the local population; bribery worked as well on the outside as it did within the ghetto. The reply if any did, would come through the official channels – written in code – as instructed.*

\*

Meier's hand rested on top of hers, and it was like an unwanted jolt of electricity. She swallowed her fear, her heart thudding painfully. 'Let's see it,' he said, softly, and she opened her hand at last, her legs turning to jelly. Meier stood too close, and she could smell him. It was sweet, yet slightly acrid. He took the ring from her palm, his fingers lingering against her rough skin, tickling. Then he brought the ring to his eye line, so that the faded gold sparkled in the low light of the warehouse. He gave a low whistle. 'Might be worth a little something, here,' he said, then to her shock put it back into her hand, closing it with his own. 'Don't you think?' he asked, his gaze raking hers meaningfully. She nodded, and he touched her face, her short hair, her lips. 'Give us a smile, Bette Davis,' he said, and Sofie did.

He winked at her, then turned to leave. 'If you're nice to me, I'll be nice back,' he promised.

Sofie's legs almost gave out as she watched him leave. She found it hard to calm her breathing. She could have been shot for being caught stealing. She closed her eyes. Her life was in his hands. How long before he tried to call in the favour?

# EIGHT

Eva kept more photographs that she found sorting through the coats in the warehouse. She had a small pile of just six that she kept in the thin mattress in her bunk: smiling mothers and laughing sons and daughters, happy couples, a woman with a polka dot scarf and a baby pressed against her cheek, a boy on a wooden horse.

'Why keep them?' asked Sofie, as Eva looked at them late at night, her memory conjuring more than the darkness would permit. 'It's not like they are worth anything.'

Eva turned to protest, then started to cough. She hoped she wasn't getting sick, though it was sometimes unavoidable here with the lack of sanitation. She couldn't remember the last time she'd seen soap. Her friend rubbed her back, both as a comfort and a gesture of peace.

'Apart from their sentimental value for the people they used to belong to, of course. What are they to *you*, Eva? If the guards found you with these you could be killed. They might think you are planning on doing something with them.'

She hadn't told Eva about what had happened with the ring, with Meier, she didn't know if it was dangerous to share it or not. But the secret twisted like a knife.

Eva snorted. 'Like what? There's so few.'

Sofie shrugged. 'I don't know – maybe tell people outside what they are doing here?'

'If I managed to get outside that would be a miracle – and I'm sure the barbed wire and electric fencing tells people all they need to know.'

Sofie leant her head against the wall of the bunk, and sighed, rubbing her neck. They were working them long hours, and Meier's constant watchful, hungry gaze was taking its toll. She longed to ask him about Lotte, but she was worried about what owing him a favour like that might cost, especially given her debt already for turning a blind eye to her theft. 'Yes, but they don't know what goes on, not really, I think they think it's just some sort of holding camp.'

Eva raised a brow. 'You don't think people know by now what it really is?'

The words *death camp* lay heavy in the air: the full weight, and the full horror of it all, unspoken, yet oppressive.

Sofie sighed, then rubbed her dark eyes. There were deep shadows beneath them. 'Honestly, I don't know if they do, or if they even care, Eva. Sometimes, I think… I hope they know what's happening here – at other times, I hope they don't, and that's the reason that it has been allowed to go on so long. The alternative – that they know, and let it happen – is unbearable.'

Eva nodded. She looked at her friend and felt the familiar stab of guilt. She swallowed. 'Sofie, if only I hadn't—'

Sofie's dark eyes snapped open, and she shot her an admonishing look. 'Don't start that again, *Kritzelei*.'

'But Sof—'

'I'm glad I followed you, all right, so leave it.'

Eva shook her head. She had been much safer back in Terezín. It was her fault that they were here now.

Sofie reached for her hand, closed her eyes again, resting her head against Eva's shoulder. 'You wouldn't have been able to stop me, *Kritzelei*, for all your tricks. Besides I didn't just follow you – I had to know if it was true, if Lotte really is here, if I could find out at last what she did with my son.'

Eva nodded. The memory of that day washing over her. It had begun with finding out where they had taken Michal first.

*

*'Auschwitz.'*

*Eva had stared at him, her hazel eyes huge. 'Are you sure?'*

*Her uncle was solemn. 'I'm afraid so.'*

*She breathed out, not taking in the surrounds. It had taken nearly a year in Terezín to find out. A year and her wedding ring – which she'd hidden well so the guards hadn't been able to find it when they arrived – as a payment to a man who worked in the record office. Her uncle had arranged it.*

*Bedrich's hand caught hold of her arm, his eyes worried. 'Don't do anything stupid, dítě, please.'*

*She looked away. Too late. She'd already decided – she'd decided a long time ago that she would follow as soon as she could.*

*'I can't promise that, uncle. I'm sorry.'*

\*

*She'd found Sofie waiting for her in the women's quarters, her dark eyes knowing. She didn't bother with a greeting, just pursed her lips and declared, 'If you're going, Kritzelei, so am I.'*

*Eva had shaken her head, unwinding the scarf that she'd tied around her long, dark hair, against the cold. 'No, Sofie, you shouldn't. It might be worse than here, probably is – I've heard some of the rumours – it's not like this place.'*

*Sofie crossed her arms, and a lock of long, dark blonde hair fell across her face, so that Eva could see the thick scars on her forehead reaching to the back of her scalp.*

*'You don't think I know about worse?' she muttered.*

*Eva sighed. 'I know you do – you told me about the camp you were in before this.'*

*Sofie rolled her eyes, and scoffed. 'That was nothing. I told you about the people who I met who'd spent time in labour camps. Westerbork was much like this, but they aren't all so marvellous, trust me, the things I've heard…'*

There was an old woman sitting behind them on a bed, darning socks. She made a disbelieving sound at the back of her throat at the idea of calling this place 'marvellous'. There was the constant hunger, fleas, bedbugs, overcrowding, disease and degradation with the overwhelming stench of human waste as the town groaned under the weight of far more people than it was ever intended to house before the Nazis transformed it into a camp. Still, even so, they knew or had heard rumours of worse.

Sofie whispered, 'It's true – I've heard things.'

Eva sighed. 'Exactly, I won't put your life at risk for mine. Okay?'

Sofie shook her head. 'You won't be, trust me – I'll be risking my life to go after my cousin – I got word that that is where they most likely sent Lotte.'

Eva's mouth opened and closed. 'When?'

'A little while ago – I finally got a response to my letter, the one you managed to send for me.'

It was a week, to be exact, and she'd been trying to decide if she should just volunteer to go. The reply from one of Lotte's friends had been short and coded, as it needed to pass beneath the authorities' gaze.

All it said was that Lotte had been put on a train and sent somewhere east, somewhere in Poland. A town called Oświęcim, she thought. Sofie had heard that it was a code for Auschwitz.

'My life is at risk all the time. It has been for years, without me having any say in it. This way I get some choice in the matter, and

I might manage to track down Lotte so that she can tell me what she did with my son – where she placed him, if I don't throttle her with my bare hands first.'

Eva had touched her friend's arm. 'But you could find out another way, go back to Lotte's neighbourhood, ask questions when the war is over… someone should know, Sofie – you don't need to follow her there.'

They had discussed it at length, what they would do when the war was over. 'It would be much safer for you to wait the war out here if you can, you know that.'

Sofie sighed. 'Maybe. But if she is there – then I will find out for sure, it might be my only chance, Kritzelei. Lotte wasn't an idiot and she wouldn't have made it obvious where she'd taken him, in order to protect him. She might have betrayed me, but she did love my child. Besides, I can't stay here without you.'

'Of course you can. You're tough – far tougher than me!'

Sofie grabbed her shoulder, roughly. 'That's why you need me, idiot. I have to come to make sure that my foolish, daydreaming friend stays alive, that we get out of this together!'

Eva laughed, then embraced her fiercely. 'I'm tougher now, you know that.'

'That's true – although your version of being tough borders on being reckless, Kritzelei, I'm coming – so don't try one of your tricks, if you go to the toilet, the kitchen, anywhere alone, I'm coming with you to make sure you don't get on that train without me, do you understand?'

*Eva shook her head. It was exactly what she'd planned on doing before she'd run into Sofie. 'How can I meet your son, Tomas, at last, only to tell him that we risked our lives because we wanted to go on some fool's mission?'*

*Sofie had taken her hand and said, 'We will explain that it was my best chance of finding out where my cousin had put him. And,* Kritzelei, *if it comes to that – this will all just be a memory, of the time his mother met her best friend.'*

*Eva had squeezed her hand back, there hadn't been much more to say after that.*

\*

Eva closed her eyes now as she lay in the bunk, listening to the sound of hundreds of other women sleeping and arguing and clinging on to life around her. There was still a part of her that wished that she had lied to Sofie – that she had come up with some other plan to distract her friend, so that Sofie could have been spared this place. She was no closer to finding Lotte than she was Michal. Had they risked it all for nothing?

Perhaps Sofie could read her mind because she opened her eyes and said, 'I still think that, *Kritzelei.* That we'll get through this and pick up our lives again, I have hope, because of you.'

It was true, before she'd met Eva, Sofie had been in a dark, dark place. But through meeting her she'd started to see a way out. Started to imagine that things might end differently.

Eva looked at her, and touched her arm. Even when everyone told her that she was mad to think the way she did, that hope was the reserve of fools, she couldn't shake hers. She looked at her friend, and said, 'But that's why I'm keeping these, see,' meaning the photographs.

Sofie frowned. 'I don't understand – so you are planning on showing them to people?'

'No, not that. Although maybe yes if we get through this. But for now, I just can't bear the thought of leaving these people behind, as if none of them mattered. This way, I don't know, they can matter to someone, they can mean something even if it is just to me.'

'Oh Eva.'

Eva shrugged. She knew that her friend was probably just thinking that she was being her usual rose-tinted self, but it was important to her – on some deep, human level – that she wasn't willing to let go of, even if it risked her survival. She put the photographs back under the far too thin mattress. 'I know it's silly in a way, but I just couldn't bear to have them burnt. I don't know if they do burn them but that's what one of the other women suggested might happen to them. What if it was Tomas or Michal?'

Sofie's dark eyes were incredulous. 'I wouldn't want anyone to risk their life for my *picture*!'

'Of course, but what if that's all there is left? People have lost everything – their belongings, their families, their identity.'

She touched her arm where the tattoo they had etched into her skin – designed to take away the essence of who she had been, and replace it with a number – was, and then started to cough, a dry thin and rasping sound.

'That's sounding worse,' said Sofie, looking at her critically, coming forward to touch her forehead. 'Have you got a fever?'

'No,' Eva lied, shrugging her hand away.

'Eva?' Sofie didn't sound convinced. She sounded worried, and suddenly on high alert, despite her fatigue.

'I'm fine, it's just a small cold, don't worry,' mumbled Eva, turning away from her friend's anxious eyes.

'Eva?'

'I'll be all right, trust me.'

# NINE

But she wasn't all right. Eva was half delirious by the morning.

'Get up. I'm taking you to the hospital,' said Sofie, shaking her arm.

'No,' Eva moaned, curling herself into a ball, wanting to stay in bed forever. It was warm, and Michal's arms were wrapped around her, her head on the spot on his shoulder which had been made just for her.

'Let's stay longer. I'll make us breakfast, we can have it in bed,' muttered Eva, her eyes closed. 'Take the day off…'

'That would be nice,' snorted Sofie despite herself. 'But come on now, wake up. Quickly.'

Eva prised open swollen lids. Her eyes felt like they had been scratched by glass and pasted back into her sockets with glue. Her tongue was thick, and it felt like her head was under water. She groaned and turned over to go back to sleep.

'Come on,' insisted Sofie. 'It's the *Appell*, they've already called us.'

Eva swung out of bed, slowly. Then she bent down and took the photographs from the bunk, and shoved them into her underwear.

'Leave those! Come on, quickly! The guard is already there! Put on your shoes,' hissed Sofie, coming forward to help her.

Eva pushed her away. 'No, I'm hot.'

'Don't be silly, it's snowing,' exclaimed Vanda, shooting Sofie a worried look.

Sofie felt Eva's forehead and closed her eyes. 'I think it might be typhus, God help her. It's been going around here like wildfire – the water is filthy,' she muttered, clenching her jaw.

Vanda helped Eva stand. 'I'll hold her up on my side, you do the same – they won't see that she's sick, I promise.'

Sofie grabbed her roughly. 'Promise me – don't drop her, they'll kill her if she can't stand.'

Vanda scowled at Sofie, and hissed, 'I know that, I'm not an idiot, she's my friend too!'

Eva patted their shoulders. 'Don't be silly, I'm fine,' she said sliding out of bed, and falling over on her weak jelly legs.

They lifted her to her feet, and between them managed to slowly drag her outside into the freezing snow. For Eva, the cold air was a temporary relief but it still couldn't cool down the fever burning through her limbs. They stood, holding her up for over two hours, arms aching, backs tensing in pain. Just the day before they had heard, more than seen, Hinterschloss shoot someone whose coughing had been getting on his nerves. When he'd walked past them, he'd held his head, then winked at them as a body was dragged away in the snow, which turned pink from the blood. 'That's better. I had such a headache.'

Hinterschloss stared at them now, pale grey eyes looking into a sea of dirty, thin faces.

He was passing by Eva, when he suddenly stopped, an odd look on his face. 'The translator,' he said, narrowing his eyes, noting her colour, her glazed eyes. 'Let me look at you. Step forward.'

Adrenalin mixed with pure fear seized hold of Eva's body and she stepped forward on her weak legs.

'Are you well?' he said, almost kindly. His voice was soft, causing the hairs on her neck to stand on end.

'I am, yes.'

He stared, his hand making a movement as if he wanted to touch her forehead but thought better of it in case it sullied him. After some time, he put his head to one side, and said, 'You look feverish.'

'Just my colouring, sir.'

He seemed to find this amusing; he laughed, eyes glinting in the wintry light. 'You feel healthy?'

'Yes, sir.'

'That's good, we like healthy workers, don't we?' he asked Meier – who nodded.

Hinterschloss shrugged, giving the other a sly smile. 'Dead or alive, makes no difference to me.' Then he turned and glared at Eva, 'I don't like liars though – they waste time.' He sniffed. 'You can understand that some people say they are healthy when they are not? Taking up valuable space that could be used by others?'

Eva didn't blink, just repeated. 'I am well, sir.'

He raised a brow, and edged nearer so that she could smell his stale, whisky breath. 'If you are indeed so healthy, as you say, then you wouldn't mind standing here for another hour?' She nodded quickly, and his smiled widened. 'Not so fast,' he said. 'Can't make it too easy you understand.' Then he bent down and picked up a large rock from the snow-covered ground. 'Raise this high above your head.'

Eva's legs shook as she stepped forward to take it. Hinterschloss gave her a satisfied smile, his hand playing with the butt of his gun. 'A little proof sometimes is necessary, do you agree?'

Meier looked down at the ground, a frown between his eyes. 'Yes,' said Eva, simply.

It was, alas, a regular form of torment, one that some of the *Kapos* performed on the other women – making them stand even longer in the cold, and devising ways of testing their fitness, or attempting to break their spirit for some imaginary slight, usually with the waste bucket above their head.

Eva struggled to lift the rock. She tensed her jaw, feeling nauseous. Sofie hesitated, stepping forward to help, and Meier shot her a cautionary look. 'Leave her, let her do it herself.'

Hinterschloss nodded, as if he approved.

'I'm fine,' said Eva to Sofie, gritting her teeth and raising the rock above her head, fighting. Her arms and legs shook as she stared ahead, past Hinterschloss's dead eyes, at the golden crest on his uniform, and thought of Michal.

*

*She would always remember the colour gold from the moment she knew she was in love. It was the colour of late summer, and early evening, the sun in her eyes, reflected off the river in her family's country home deep in the mountains. A shadow passed over her and she looked up from the otter she was sketching, and sunlight blinded her, bright and gold. She cupped her hand to shade her eyes and when her vision cleared, there he was.*

*A dimple in his cheek, as he knelt down, shifting the source of light, from gold to green and back again.*

*'Michal,' she'd breathed in wonder.*

*He nodded, his mouth forming a soft smile, as he stared at her.*

*'You're here?'*

*He nodded. 'I couldn't stay in Prague.'*

*She'd stared, marvelling at the sight of him, here with her. 'Why not?'*

*'Because you weren't there.'*

*Happiness, pure and champagne bright, had bubbled up inside when he'd kissed her.*

*

Hinterschloss stared at her, while her eyes glazed over as she fixed on the distance, her arms above her head. She focussed only on breathing in and out and picturing Michal's beloved face, his curls, the dimple showing in his cheek.

Eva wasn't sure how long she stood there, lost in the past. Black spots danced before her eyes and she fought the overwhelming pull of delirium, which was growing stronger at every passing moment. She was beginning to wonder what was real and what wasn't. Dancing at the corner of her eyes were her family. Her mother with that soft, encouraging smile of hers. Her cousin Mila laughing as she ran by the lake in her red bathing costume, dark blonde locks flying behind her. Then, in the distance, she thought she saw her uncle Bedrich – only he was here, in Auschwitz. He was wearing his roguish grey hat, and walking that ambling gait of his, a slow smile creeping on his craggy face. He raised a finger and motioned for her to keep going, keep holding on.

Was it real? Was he here?

She wet her lips, and breathed out his name, 'Uncle Bedrich?' but they were cracked, her mouth dry and parched and no sound escaped. Her arms shook, but still she stood.

An hour passed, and finally Hinterschloss appeared appeased. He sniffed as he looked down at her; everyone else was getting restless, and his own belly was starting to rumble. He spat near her feet and sneered, 'All right, translator. Clear to work.'

Eva nodded, then slowly dropped the rock – only when he'd gone past did she step backwards, and half fall into Sofie's waiting arms, which supported her on the long, interminable walk to the warehouses. At some point she passed out and her friend tapped her face gently to wake her up long enough for them to walk inside.

What little energy she might have had left had been stolen by Hinterschloss's evil game with the rock. It was soon apparent that Eva wouldn't be able to do much sorting that day, as she was so delirious she was barely able to stand. Worse, it seemed like every time they turned, a guard was watching them.

Sofie managed to get her into her section by asking Meier if it would be all right, and he'd agreed. Although having the guard so close by was worrisome, it was better than risking Eva collapsing near Hinterschloss.

Eva found herself falling asleep on a pile of bedding, and when Sofie heard the sound of heavy boots, she managed to pile them on top of her just in time.

'Wasn't there another girl?' asked a guard called Skelter coming to check.

'She went to the latrine,' said Sofie. 'Meier said she could.'

He checked his watch. There were three bathroom breaks a day.

'Fine. Make sure you ask *me* next time, and see that she's back here faster. I don't pay you to take breaks.'

Sofie nodded. 'I will.'

Beneath her pile of coats, Eva began to mutter that they didn't pay them, but Sofie's hand slipped beneath the pile as fast as she could and into her mouth.

'What was that?' asked the guard, turning to come inside the room and inspect it.

Sofie shrugged. 'Just a rat, sir – sometimes they hide in the coats. We found one the other day the size of a *cat*.'

The guard wrinkled his nose in distaste, and stepped back quickly through the door.

'See that she is back here,' he ordered.

Sofie inclined her head.

When he'd left, she pulled Eva out from under the large pile of the coats. 'Come on, I'm taking you to the hospital.'

'No,' Eva moaned. 'Not there. They kill people there, they don't heal them. That's what everyone says, especially if you're Jewish.'

'We have no choice, Eva, if it's typhus you're dead without medication – besides if they catch you like this, you will definitely get killed. Skelter is already suspicious.'

Eva shook her head, but when she tried to stand up she was so delirious that she thought she was back in Terezín. 'Uncle Bedrich,' she slurred. 'Why did you let Papa get on that transport, you could have stopped him…' Then suddenly she smiled sadly. 'Darling, don't you want to take your violin, surely you'll still be able to play?'

Somehow, Sofie managed to get her out the building, and when Meier stopped her she said she was taking her friend to the hospital.

'The hospital?' he said. 'So she is sick?'

'Yes, she needs to go, now, please I'm worried about her.'

He nodded, his face softening. 'All right, let me help you,' and he slung Eva's arm over his shoulder.

Sofie breathed a sigh of relief. Together they half carried Eva to the medical barracks, which had grown over a compound of buildings.

Meier spoke to one of the doctors and they were directed to a waiting room. When he turned to leave, he gave Sofie's hand a surreptitious squeeze.

'You might have to pay for this,' said Eva, having a moment of lucidity in her fear.

'Let me worry about that,' said Sofie firmly.

The hospital barracks looked like a regular medical facility, with doctors wearing lab coats, and consulting charts. Sofie and Eva sat in the waiting room, and once they were called, a Slovakian nurse checked Eva over.

'They kill us here,' Eva repeated, eyes glazed, her head tossing from side to side as masked doctors with bloodstained aprons advanced on her, a product of her delirious, panic-filled mind.

'No,' said Sofie, denying it. 'You're safe, *Kritzelei*.'

'Is it typhus?' she asked the nurse – who nodded.

'I think so – a bad case too.'

As her friend worried over her fate, Eva stared at Sofie, and her delirium changed again, she was back in their bunk trying to make her feel better; telling her friend the stories she liked to hear. She began in her mind to tell her about her first date with Michal. But, of course, no words escaped her parched lips, as she slipped into the memory, like a comforting robe on cold shoulders.

# TEN

## Prague, April 1938

The Smetana Hall was grand. The beautiful art nouveau decor offered a stained-glass ceiling, impressive Slavic paintings and gilded lamps, which shone down on the rapt audience, all of whom were following the movement of the concert master intensely.

But as the sound of Rachmaninoff's violin concerto swelled the hall, Eva's eyes were drawn to a pair of shoes seated in the first-row violins.

The shoes were black, with worn patches that showed up like bald spots despite the polish. Eva stared at them in delight, then looked up at the young man who was sitting in the front. He had curly brown hair and light eyes, and even before she saw the dimples in his cheeks – when he grinned down at her, as if he knew exactly who she was – she knew she was in trouble.

*

In the lobby, her mother was getting their coats, when she felt a tap on her shoulder, and she turned around to see him.

*His eyes were green, she realised. A vivid shade, like a dappled glade.*

*'You came,' he said, his lips curved so that there was a slight dimple in his cheek.*

*She swallowed, resisting the urge to pat her dark hair which had been loosely curled by her cousin Mila, so that it rested on her shoulders.*

*'I did,' she replied, hardly able to help her smile.*

*He returned it, showing very even teeth, and she felt her stomach skip – like she'd drunk champagne or spun around the room – as the world suddenly sped up, just a little too fast, full of life and noise and colour. She took in a breath, but nothing seemed to slow.*

*'Would you like to go for a walk?'*

*She stared back at the tall, handsome stranger with his old, worn shoes, and laughing eyes, and blinked in surprise. 'What, now?'*

*He shrugged, and the dimple deepened. 'The city is beautiful at night.'*

*She bit her lip, but couldn't help the wide smile stretching across her face. 'Give me a second,' she breathed, then ran back to her mother to tell her. She came back a few moments later with her mother's admonishments, along with her laughter ringing in her ears.*

*He raised a brow, green eyes dancing, perhaps slightly amazed that she had agreed, because he teased, 'You know, I could be anyone, what if you were running off with a madman or something?'*

*Eva shook her head, dark curls bouncing. 'See that woman back there,' she said, pointing an arm to a tall and elegant woman – a flash of gold about her throat, pearl earrings glinting against her dark chignon – standing speaking to the maestro, who she had somehow cornered, and who was looking oddly small as he listened to her. 'That is my mother, Anka Copco. By now, she will know your address, middle name, and where she should send the police if I'm not home by twelve.'*

*He let out a deep laugh. 'She sounds formidable.'*

*Eva nodded, then grinned. 'She is. She told me that although I have just turned twenty-one, she will still be obeyed or there will be consequences.' She shrugged. 'I suppose it's what most mothers do.'*

*'Not mine,' he said, inclining his head in a respectful way. 'Mine let me do what I liked, but that wasn't always a good thing,' he winked. Then he straightened, looking down at her. 'So that's Anka Copco,' he said, his eyes twinkling. 'And who is her daughter?'*

*Eva coloured. 'Eva.'*

*'Pleased to meet you at last, peach-girl. I am Michal Adami.'*

# ELEVEN

Eva had one of the worst cases of epidemic typhus the nurses had seen. Her body was covered in a rash, and she was in the grips of a dangerous fever. The delirium was the most worrisome sign as it indicated the severity of her illness. Typhus had claimed many lives in the camps, but if treated the recovery could be quite fast.

Sofie watched as the nurse forced her friend to swallow the antibiotics. She wanted nothing more than to wait by her side and see how she did, but she knew that if she didn't get back there would be questions.

When she returned to the Kanada, Meier was waiting for her. She could see that he was pleased that he had found a way to get closer to her – by helping her friend.

'How is she?' he asked, putting a hand on her shoulder. Sofie had to fight the urge to shake his hand away. There was a sweet smell from his breath, slightly sickly, like burnt vanilla. Instead of pulling away, she swallowed, then put her hand over his, touching it briefly. 'The nurse said it's a bad case, I just hope she can pull through it.' She looked up at him. 'If only I could be there – stay by her side.'

They were standing in the shadows, near a large pile of bedding, and she looked up to make sure that there was no one looking, then she turned and kissed him briefly on the lips.

His eyes widened in delight, and he cupped her face, kissing her back, harder. Sofie let him. Closing her mind to the smell of burnt vanilla, which flooded her senses, making her feel faintly nauseated.

Finally, he squeezed her tight, mistaking the tears in her eyes for worry for her friend. He wiped a finger beneath her lashes. 'I can arrange that, I'll do what I can for my girl.'

Sofie looked at him, her dark eyes not giving anything away. 'You are my girl, aren't you?'

Sofie looked away for a moment, then nodded. She gave him another quick, surreptitious kiss, a forced smile on her face, which he didn't notice. 'I could be, yes.'

This seemed to make him very happy. 'Good.'

Meier arranged it so that Sofie could stay with her friend for the rest of the day, and she watched over Eva as she thrashed on a hospital bed, her face bone white, her lips dry and chapped.

There was nothing to do but wait and hope the fever would break. Meier escorted Sofie back to the hospital over the next few days so that she could see her friend for a few minutes at a time. It took two full days for the fever to break, and for Eva to wake up, feeling weak, starving, but clear-headed.

She watched as patients like her slept in beds, but no doctors came to check on them. She didn't know if she should attempt to leave, if it was worse for her or not. Sofie came over to check on her in the afternoon, a smile on her face. 'You had me worried there, *Kritzelei.*'

Eva pressed her friend's hand, her muscles were weak still and the pressure was light, like a butterfly. 'Thank you for everything – I hope I haven't made things worse for you.'

She meant with Meier, who it was clear now thought they were in love.

Sofie rolled her eyes. 'Don't be daft, having you dead would be much worse than dealing with that boy,' and Eva let out a small chuckle. Then she sat up slowly, her eyes scanning the room. The fear clutching hold of her once more at where she was.

'I should get back,' she said.

Sofie pushed her back down again, gently. 'Stay, rest. Meier said he will escort you back tonight.'

Eva nodded. She was still weak, and tired, it would be good to rest.

'Here, have this,' Sofie said, giving her a small wedge of black bread. Eva nodded, breaking off a large chunk in her hunger which she shoved into her mouth, but her muscles were so weak it took forever to chew.

'Thanks.'

'Course, *Kritzelei.*'

Eva nodded. 'Sorry I put you through this.' Eva meant having to look after her, risking herself.

'Don't be. I'm holding you to that promise you made on our first day.'

Eva looked at her, then gave a small smile. 'We will live?'

'We will live,' Sofie agreed.

As Eva waited in the bed, she watched as an old man with a bucket mopped the floors. His face was familiar somehow.

He caught her staring at him, and then raised two fingers at her in a greeting. He had thick bushy eyebrows and very dark eyes.

'Is it you?' she asked.

He frowned. Then shuffled forward in his striped pyjamas. 'You know me?' His accent was thick, soupy German.

He had a mole over one lip. He was thin, thinner than in the photograph she had of him.

'In a way,' she said. She bent down to fetch the small bundle of photographs she'd moved from her underwear to the folded-up roll of her far too long sleeve, and found his easily. The one of the man with the bushy eyebrows, the mole, and the shy girl and laughing boy.

She looked at it, then smiled a wide smile, for the first time in a very long while. 'It is you,' she said, in awe, and gave it to him.

His eyes bulged, and filled with tears, as he touched the photograph, with shaking fingers. 'How did you get this?'

She explained about the warehouse, about going through the men's coats and what she'd done, how she'd kept just a few of the photographs.

He blinked, touching the faces of his children. The photograph was small in his thick, gnarled fingers.

He looked up at her. 'Why did you keep it?'

She shrugged a shoulder. 'I don't know, I couldn't bear to see it burnt – there was a rumour that they did that, I didn't want to take the risk.'

He swallowed. 'Thank you.'

He looked around, in case anyone was listening, then turned back when he saw the coast was clear. 'They took my girl, Ilsa.'

'Where?' asked Eva, sitting up.

'From the train. They put the men to one side and the women. I found out later, she went left.'

Eva closed her eyes: that poor child. People who were fit and able to work – not too young or too old, were taken to the right, they could live and work, like slaves, like them. The ones who went left were killed upon arrival.

'I thought I would never see her again,' he said, shaking his head in disbelief.

Eva frowned, until she realised he was talking about the photograph.

'Thank you,' he said, touching her arm.

Eva felt something warm and light enter her chest as if the weight of this place had lifted for a moment – the feeling was wondrous.

She smiled, shook her head. 'I can't believe I found you – out of all the people here.'

He nodded. 'It's a miracle,' he agreed. 'And I must admit I had given up on those. There's hundreds of thousands of people here. If you had tried to look for me it would have taken you many months.'

She nodded. It was pure chance, pure luck.

'Can I – is there anything I can do for you in return?' he asked.

That's the way it worked in the camp. It wasn't a bad thing, favours were the only thing you could offer, the only currency that could end up improving things slightly.

She nodded. It wasn't time to pretend that she was above that sort of thing, no one was. A nurse would be here soon and then he'd have to leave, he was one of the few male prisoners she'd seen in months, and the only one she'd spoken to.

'My husband, Michal Adami. I need to know if he's alive.'

The light in his eyes dimmed slightly. 'Like I said, there's so many people, I don't know if I'll be able to find out.'

He didn't explain that every woman he met asked him the same thing, and more often than not, without even needing to ask, the answer was that they were dead. And if they were alive, it would be like trying to find a needle in a haystack.

She grabbed his arm, the one with his tattoo, covering it with hers. 'What's your name?'

'Herman.'

'Eva.'

'I believe in luck, despite everything. Look at us, Herman, if that wasn't luck, I don't know what is, and a little is all we need.'

He nodded. 'Eva, we will need all the help we can get. A few more prayers couldn't hurt. How will I find you?' he asked.

'I'll find a way to come back here.'

She wasn't sure how just yet.

He nodded, then smiled, touched the pocket of his pyjamas where he'd put the photograph, a gesture of farewell, then he was gone.

'You think he will find Michal, truly?' asked Sofie on the first night Eva was back in her familiar bunk, after she'd told them about what had happened.

'I don't know. I have to hope.'

No one said that it was unlikely, they didn't have to. They had all lost husbands and brothers, fathers and sons. Very few of them knew who was alive or not in here; but then, the chances of Eva finding the man with the moustache in the tiny bundle of photographs she had found had been slim to nothing.

'I could ask Meier – maybe he knows something, or could find out.'

Eva shook her head. 'He's friends with Hinterschloss. I think if somehow Meier let it slip that he was looking for my husband, he'd kill him, just to spite me.'

Sofie bit her lip. It was all too likely, she hadn't thought of that, and was glad that she hadn't asked him yet. She'd wanted to be sure if she could trust him or not before she asked after Lotte and Michal. Meier was better than some of the other guards, but he was young and naive, and had already made the mistake of letting Hinterschloss know how he felt about Sofie, when he told him that he thought she looked like the film star Bette Davis. To the point that the other guard now made it his mission to touch her whenever he did the *Appell*.

'Just testing the merchandise, I don't like it when my friends get a better share.' Then he'd sneered. 'I think he can keep these little plums though.'

But it hadn't stopped him from doing it again.

Sofie tried not to think of it, of them. 'I still can't believe you found the man in the photograph, and that was all he had left of his daughter,' she said.

Eva nodded.

'Maybe you weren't so mad after all, *Kritzelei*, for keeping them,' said Sofie with a smile. 'Maybe others will try to get theirs back too.'

Eva smiled back. 'I doubt it.'

But Sofie was right. After she'd given Herman back his photograph, she began to see on her way to the Kanada – by accident or design, she wasn't sure which – more men by the fence calling out to her, wanting to know if she had their photographs. But of course she only had the tiniest handful. That she'd had Herman's was more than likely a one-off, a miracle really.

Sometimes it was possible to snatch a few seconds to speak to them through the fence, before anyone noticed.

'Here,' said an older man with greying hair and large blue eyes, pushing through a small piece of sausage from the fence.

'But I might not have your photograph, I only kept a very few,' she explained.

He shook his head. 'No, I know. I didn't keep any, I wish I did, that's the thing – I was always too busy working. That's what I thought a husband and father should do – provide.' His face looked sad. 'My wife arranged for a professional photographer to come one morning for a family portrait. It was a Saturday, and I was annoyed, I had stuff to do at the office, so I left. I regret that now.'

Eva didn't know what to say. There had been so many moments they had all taken for granted, thinking they had all the time in the world. There were so many things she wished she could have done better too.

'Your family knew you loved them, that's why you worked so hard.'

His eyes filled. 'You think so?'

She wiped away a tear from her own. 'I do.'

He cleared his throat, fighting sudden tears. 'Anyway. Here, have the sausage. It was such a nice thing you did, keeping Herman's photo like that, he's my friend. Eat, please.'

Eva nodded, and slipped the piece of sausage between her teeth and chewed; it was delicious. 'Thank you.'

'Can you tell me what your husband looks like?' he asked.

'He's tall, with curly brown hair and green eyes.'

'No one has curly hair here,' he said. Eva's heart plummeted, and he waved a hand in dismissal as he explained. 'They shaved us all.'

'Oh,' said Eva. 'Of course.' It was some time before her heartbeat returned to normal.

'Do you have a photograph of him? We could circulate it, someone might have seen him?'

She shook her head, his was one of the photographs she didn't have.

He nodded. 'It's okay. Don't worry, we'll still ask around.'

She looked at him. 'I could draw him, if I could get paper, a pen.'

'Here?' He widened his eyes, then nodded. 'I don't know if I'd be able to get that. I'll try though.'

'Thanks.'

*

Over the course of the next few weeks – despite her belief that it wouldn't happen again – she managed to track down another one of the men with families from the photographs by the way he'd described his wife's dotted scarf, and laughing eyes.

It was heartbreaking to see the man behind the fence begin to cry. 'She died on the train with me. We were lucky though, before we were taken, we'd got word that our son made it safely to London with my sister, can you believe that – he's there learning English?' he smiled at the thought, 'Maybe even reciting Shakespeare already, eh?'

Eva smiled. That was a nice thought.

'I will keep this for him,' said the man.

She nodded, turned to leave, tears in her eyes.

She was happy to return the handful of photographs she'd kept, but she wished more than anything that she could return the people within them to the past before everything was torn from their lives.


'You, photo-girl! Eva.'

Eva turned as she was on her way into the Kanada, to see Herman. She looked quickly over her shoulder to see if any of the guards were watching and sidled closer to the fence. 'Herman, hello! You have news? Have you found Michal?' she asked, quickly, breathlessly.

He shook his head.

Her heart sank, but she reminded herself that no news was good news.

'No, not yet. But we got you this. It might help?' She looked down and saw in his old liver-spotted hand a small scrap of yellowing paper, and a tiny stub of a pencil. In this place, it was like gold, and if you were caught with it the sentence was death.

She took it from him quickly, her months of sleight of hand practice with her uncle Bedrich made quick work of hiding the items up her sleeve. 'Thank you,' she breathed.

'If you can draw a portrait, I'll be here tomorrow, the same time, to fetch it.'

She nodded. She could do that.

'Try to make it as accurate as possible.'

Michal's face was etched inside her heart, it would be no trouble.

# TWELVE

Sofie had found a way to get away from Meier – and thus the increasing, unwarranted attention she was receiving from Hinterschloss, and she grabbed at it quickly.

Sara, their *Kapo*, had come in after speaking to one of the doctors outside, wanting to know if any of them had nursing experience, as there was a shortage. There was a new doctor, named Mengele, someone who would be very busy, and they needed as many personnel as they could find. In the weeks to come she would come to realise that the good-looking, well-groomed doctor was the very incarnation of evil, and of Auschwitz, but at that moment she hadn't known any of this. All she'd seen was a chance to get away from Meier.

'I do,' said Sofie, to Eva's surprise, which she tried to hide when Sara turned to look at her.

Sara furrowed a brow. 'Really? If you are lying you know they will kill you?' she said.

Eva had watched her friend swallow.

'I have experience – five years in Vienna.'

The *Kapo* nodded. 'Good, they need you there now. Some big case. They said you could stay here for now, though you might get moved on to another barrack with the other staff later.'

When Sofie came back in the early hours of the morning, she snuggled next to Eva.

'How did it go?' Eva asked.

'It was fine, I think I fooled them. But how long, *Kritzelei*, before they find out that where I worked wasn't in a human hospital?' she whispered. 'And only as a teenager?'

*

*As a child, Sofie had dreamt of becoming a veterinarian. She loved animals, and her favourite place to visit in Austria was the zoo, where she would watch the orangutans, the elephants and the Siberian tigers. In her small flat which she shared with her father, above his watchmaking shop in the centre of Leopoldstadt, the Jewish quarter – which had been home to her family for over three generations – she had adopted a little menagerie herself, including a small feather duster of a dog, named Boopshi, as well as several nameless stray cats who were collectively called 'Shoo' by her allergic father, and a tortoise, named Freud.*

*When she was fourteen she began volunteering at the Schönbrunn Zoo, the world's oldest zoo, which had once belonged to the emperor of Lorraine. It was a forty-five-minute train ride and she would rush there after school for the briefest of visits, but it was* worth it to clean up the pens of elephants and tigers. Her father, Carl, often joked that Sofie liked animals better than people. Sometimes she thought he was right. Animals didn't pretend. They were simpler, and much nicer at times.

In any case, he was wrong in one respect, she liked the people she knew. Like her maternal grandparents, who lived in a beautiful apartment around the corner, who she stayed with every Friday for Shabbat dinner.

She liked plaiting the dough for the challah in the morning with her grandmother, and watching the bread come out of the oven, polishing the silver, and laying the table with the Shabbat candles, which were only lit after sundown. It was always a fine table, with fresh flowers from the market, and always a dessert or two, usually home-made apple strudel or cheesecake, which was her grandfather's speciality.

When she turned seventeen she began training as a veterinary nurse, and met another student, named Lucas. He was a kind soul who, like her, preferred animals to humans. It wasn't a great love. More of a summer romance, but unfortunately by the end of it, it was one in which she was left rather compromised, with the result that she was pregnant. A fact she realised long after the short-lived romance had fizzled out.

Lucas offered to do the honourable thing, even though by now, a few months later, he had given his heart to another, but Sofie refused. Despite the scandal, and the disappointment and shame she would be bringing onto her family, she couldn't commit herself to a life with a man she didn't love.

'You're being far too idealistic,' her father had reprimanded her after she'd told him the news, shaking his head at her in his disappointment. Then he put his head in his hands and wished once more that his wife had lived long enough to help raise her. 'I let you go wild – your mother would have known what to do – she would have told you about these things!' It was a frequent lament. He looked at her and sighed. 'She would have prepared you better, explained properly about men.'

Despite herself, Sofie had laughed, her dark eyes alight. 'Oh, Papa, that has been explained to me, a lot – by Granny – and Lucas wasn't like that, we should have known better, I do know that. Especially now. But I just don't see how marrying him would make this situation any better.'

Her father had stared at her in amazement, his eyes huge, as if the answer was obvious.

'He could provide a life for you – and the child.'

Sofie had frowned, crossing her arms, and Boopshi jumped into her lap. Sofie stroked his wiry fur. 'Are you kicking me out of the house?'

He blinked. 'No, of course not.'

She stared at him, eyes penetrating. 'Then I don't understand – is it that I would be a burden?'

Sofie was perhaps always a little too blunt. She didn't believe in wasting time sugar-coating things. She couldn't really see how she would be a burden as the shop did well, and they didn't live extravagant lives.

*Her father pinched the bridge of his nose, not sure how to explain that marriage was often the right thing to do, even if it's not what one wanted. 'That's not what I mean – you know this is your home, always. I'm worried about what people will think, Sofie.'*

*She gave him a look. 'Well, don't.'*

*He shook his head. 'It's not that simple!'*

*Sofie was genuinely puzzled. 'It should be. If I am free to stay here, then please let me be free to make this decision, Papa.'*

*'It's not like we can force her to marry him, can we?' her grandfather said later, sounding a little hopeful.*

*'No, unfortunately not,' agreed her father.*

*A week later though, they tried something else. Her grandmother suggested that the two women go out for a chat. She took her out to a nearby café and beseeched her over a pot of coffee the two barely touched.*

*'Look, Sofie, I know what you're saying makes sense, I have known enough young women who found themselves trapped in loveless marriages, having children with a man they don't respect. Living a life they never envisioned for themselves when they were young. I understand that, so I won't try to persuade you to change your mind on this. You've always had strong opinions, and the kind of backbone to stick with them, which you'll need now more than ever. But allow this old woman to offer you some further advice, all right?'*

Sofie nodded, taking a sip of her cold black coffee and setting it down with a grimace.

'If you have the baby here it's going to cause a fallout, for everyone, not just yourself.'

Sofie stared. 'A falling out?'

'No, a fallout – like a bomb, which sounds dramatic, I know. But trust me, this will ricochet in all our lives and cause all kinds of problems. For your father's business, for you – for the family. In this neighbourhood, we all know each other's business, unfortunately. I'd love to live in a time when an unwed woman who gets pregnant is not seen as a blot on her family or herself—'

Sofie gasped. 'But that's ridiculous, when a man does it – gets some girl pregnant…' she protested hotly, tears springing to her eyes.

Her grandmother raised a hand, and agreed. 'Nothing happens to him, not really, I know. There are a few whispers and maybe some people will make a fuss, maybe not, but that's about it. It's not fair but that's the world we live in. It's always been this way – and even if people get used to it, think of the child, raised as a bastard – being teased, being judged – you know they will.'

Sofie frowned as she considered her grandmother's words. The word 'bastard' reverberated in her skull, like a sharp stone. 'If you won't force me to marry Lucas, what then? Go and live somewhere else, is that what you're suggesting?'

Her grandmother touched her arm. 'No, well, not for long. You can go to live with your cousin Lotte in the countryside, in Bregenz, till you've had the baby. Then you can come back.'

Sofie stared, then closed her eyes in horror. 'Alone? Is that what you're implying – after I give the baby up?'

Her grandmother looked at her, her eyes serious. 'That is an option, of course.'

Sofie shook her head, and shot out of her chair, sudden, angry tears coursing down her face. 'I won't give it away!' she hissed.

'Sit down!' commanded her grandmother, as a few people stopped to stare.

Sofie stood, breathing heavily, not making a move either way.

Her grandmother sighed, and said, 'The other option, Sofie, is to have the baby there and wait.'

Sofie dashed the tears away from her eyes and took a seat. 'For how long?'

'A few months. We can say you got married, and your husband passed away – some illness or something. Then you can come back, with a ring on your finger.'

Sofie stared as her grandmother pulled off a ring from her right hand, an anniversary present from her grandfather, gold with a sapphire in an empire setting. 'Here.'

Sofie crossed her arms, and didn't take it. She hated deceit. 'I'd rather own up to my own mistakes, than pretend.'

Her grandmother shook her head, exasperated. 'You have to meet us halfway, Sofie, if not for you then for the child, at least.'

Sofie sighed, she stared at her for a long moment, then finally nodded. She figured most people would guess anyway, but if it *made them feel more comfortable with the lie, she'd let them have it for her family's sake.*

\*

*By the time Sofie came back to Vienna with her baby, Tomas, she had turned eighteen and he was six months old. Her place at the veterinary programme was gone. There was no time for studies with a new child anyway, despite the help that came rather willingly from her father and grandparents. Despite their misgivings about his parentage, they welcomed him wholeheartedly in their lives. He was a cheerful, happy baby with big brown eyes and a thick patch of dark blond hair, that her father said must have come from Sofie's mother.*

*As he grew, her father was convinced that he shared her mother's nature too. He was a gentle, sensitive soul, drawn to flowers, and music. He would sit downstairs on the floor quietly, happily playing with his toys, and making the customers smile as he laughed whenever Sofie tickled him.*

*As the months passed, she settled down into her new life as a mother. While she missed her studies, and wished that she had managed to train as a veterinary nurse, being a parent was its own adventure, and there was every chance that she could return to her studies once Tomas was older, perhaps even go further and become a veterinarian in her own right.*

*For now, she helped out at her father's shop, where she'd been an apprentice of a kind since she was six; where her head for figures and nimble fingers were just as at home fixing watches as they were changing nappies. It was fine for now, she thought, satisfied. She was young and still had her whole life ahead of her, there was still time.*

*Until, suddenly, that all changed, almost overnight, with one word:* Anschluss.

\*

Sofie looked at Eva now, and sighed, brought suddenly back into the reality of her current situation, away from the moment Austria was annexed by the Germans, as she lay next to her friend in the cold bunk, worrying about her new job posting – and what anyone would do if they found out that she hadn't really been much of a nurse at all.

'The only real experience I have is working in my father's watchmaking shop,' she said, raising her long, slim fingers. 'Sorting through cogs isn't quite the same as bone and flesh.'

'I doubt that will matter,' said Eva. 'It's not like they think of us as anything more than machines or animals anyway.'

'Especially if you are Jewish, like us,' agreed Vanda, softly, turning over to face them, a hand coming up to rub the sleep out of her pale lashes. It was true, most of the people in their barracks were Jews, and from Czechoslovakia. There were a few anomalies like Sofie who was from Austria originally, but that was because they'd been in Terezín to begin with. For the most part the camp officials thought it was safer if like stayed with like. It was easier to be with your own, they thought. But it wasn't perfect; people got moved around as they were placed on different work details, so the inevitable mixing did happen. Even so, there was a distinct hierarchy in the camp, and those with the worst status were the Jews, it was a bit better if you were half and half, with one non-Jewish parent. Political prisoners had it possibly the best, and so did the Polish, who'd been here longer.

The hospital looked like the real thing but it wasn't quite like the hospitals they knew. Eva had spent most of her time there asleep but even she saw that while doctors wore lab coats, they didn't seem to do much healing. They were busy though, very busy, although it was difficult to see with what. There were dark rumours, whispers of what happened there, though no one knew for sure. So they were interested to hear more now, from Sofie.

Sofie closed her eyes, she was tired, yet wide awake, a horrid state brought on by fear that was all too familiar, sleep if it came at all, would be much later. Thankfully hospital staff were exempt from the *Appells*. 'The care is rudimentary at best. The doctors make rounds but don't really look at patients. Of course, the nurses will treat people with typhus or something, to ensure they can get back to work fast, but from what I could tell the hospital is really for one thing only.'

'What's that?' asked Eva.

'Experiments.'

Her eyes widened, she hadn't been expecting that. 'What kind of experiments?'

'Things to help them win the war – with us as the lab rats.'

'What kind of things?'

Sofie's head swam, she could still see one of the women, who had been led away, blood pooling down her leg. They hadn't even bandaged it, and she could even see the bone as the poor woman stumbled towards a bed where a nurse took her to 'recover'. She shuddered. One of the other nurses had explained later that the new doctor, Mengele, had put something in the bone as an experiment, the purpose wasn't really explained.

'You don't really want to know.' She sighed, and whispered, 'I need something else to think about, *Kritzelei*, something *good*. Tell me about your first date with Michal, after the concert, when you went walking along the river.'

'Yes, I'd like to hear too,' said Helga, and Vanda nodded, giving up on sleep also.

So Eva did.

# THIRTEEN

## *Prague, April 1938*

*They walked through the old city on a cool April night just after the rain had fallen. Eva breathed it in; sweet and fresh, where the rain mingled with the tarmac. It was her favourite sort of night, where time seemed to stand still.*

*Along the river, they could just make out the soft lights from the boats, winking at them as they passed along the banks. Michal was far taller than her, and often had to bend down to look at her. She shivered in the cool night, and he offered her his jacket. She bit her lip as he helped slip it on, breathing in his warm, clean scent. There was just a faint hint of cologne which was pleasant and mildly spicy, and Eva couldn't help finding it slightly intoxicating. She felt her cheeks warm at the thought, and she desperately searched for something to say to the tall, handsome man walking beside her. It had been easier in the concert hall, with so many people. Safe. Out here, just the two of them, her heartbeat sounded loud in her ears.*

*'When did you learn to play the violin like that?' she asked at last.*

*He turned to look at her, his brow furrowing, slowing his naturally brisk stride to match hers. He ran a hand through his curls, as he thought back, a smile on his lips. 'When I was about four. We spent the summer with my family in Bratislava. They had this huge old house that went over several storeys, and I loved exploring its treasures – especially the attic, there were all these things stored there from a lifetime: an old rocking horse, clothes from the previous century, board games, books, but the thing that struck me most was an old red violin that I became enchanted by. I kept taking it out from its case – quite gently I suppose, despite my age – and running my fingers lightly against the strings. My mother kept looking for me, and finding me with it. My uncle was touched by this – thought it meant something,' he shrugged, laughing. His green eyes crinkled at the corners. 'He said he'd always wanted my cousin, Jakub, to take an interest in the violin but he never did. So my uncle arranged for me to have lessons. It was an indulgence, they all said. But I loved it, and after that I played every day. When I went home, my uncle gave me that old red violin, which I used until I was about sixteen and I bought a new one, better suited to my size,' he joked, indicating his long arms, and torso, 'I got it from the money I'd made playing at a little restaurant in the evenings. I told them I was twenty so that I could drink too. It took close to a year as I decided I'd get one just like Jascha Heifetz had – he's regarded as one of the best violinists in the world. I got to meet him last year, when he came here for a performance. I still have that old violin though.'*

*They walked up a street, away from the river, and she smiled, picturing the little boy he must have been and he grinned back, eyes dancing in the streetlight. 'Your turn. When did you start sketching – I saw you in the square.'*

*Her mouth fell open in surprise. 'You did?'*

*He nodded, a dimple showing in his tanned cheek.*

*She looked away towards the busy streets, where smartly dressed men and women in fashionable clothes were walking from theatres, cinemas and bars, laughter ringing throughout the air, and her heart started to beat faster.*

*He laughed. 'You're not the only one who did some spying.'*

*She looked back at him and shook her head in surprise, laughing too. As an artist, her world was all about perspective. It was strange that she hadn't considered that he could see her, but she had assumed that he was lost in his music.*

*She blushed, looked down and then answered. 'I've always drawn – my mother says that I was born with a pencil in my hand. I always have a sketchbook with me, just in case I see something that I need to capture, a moment, a memory, something unusual. You never know what you'll see.' She lifted a shoulder. It was a beautiful world, and she liked to notice it.*

*'You have your sketchbook with you, even now?' he asked, lips parting in surprise.*

*'Yes,' she said, with a small nod, patting a leather satchel, which was large and somewhat misshapen, not the sort of accessory one took to the symphony – as her mother had admonished her*

109

earlier. She didn't care though, without her sketchbook she would have felt naked, or lost.

His eyes twinkled, and he shook his head. 'So, you bring your work with you even on a date?'

She laughed, then looked up at him, eyes alight. 'I didn't realise I would be on a date.'

'I did.'

She turned to look at him in surprise. He shrugged. 'Well, see, I could see more of you than just your shoes.'

She laughed again, then shook her head. 'Come on,' she beckoned, dragging him by his hand to a bench near a streetlamp. She sat and he peered down at her, his expression puzzled, as she pulled out her sketchbook, and a pencil, which she put behind her ear, while she grinned up at him. 'I want to make a record of this night. Something tells me I'm going to want one.'

'Of what?' he asked, showing a dimple as he took a seat next to her, sitting maybe a bit closer than necessary, his leg warm alongside hers.

She took a breath, then opened her sketchbook, smoothing the page with her fingers, her hazel eyes serious, before she began. 'Of the day I met you.'

# FOURTEEN

She drew the portrait of Michal at night, on the tiny scrap of paper that Herman's friend had supplied her. It was as clear as if he were sitting before her, though she had to imagine what he looked like with shaved hair.

'Why do they need a portrait, couldn't they just ask around for his name?' said Zanda, who sat on the edge of the bunk, her bony knees tucked beneath her chin.

'Some keep their names to themselves. They become different people here, keeping their past untouched,' answered Sofie.

Eva nodded. It was true. Some of the girls in their barrack were like that. Especially the ones who had seen their families killed. It was easier to pretend you were just a number, harder to be reminded every day of who you once were. It was one of the reasons Sofie was sure she was having a hard time tracking down her cousin, Lotte.

She'd had a few red herrings, and once she'd seen someone who almost looked like her, but it wasn't her in the end. If anyone would want to hide her identity, it might be Lotte, after what she had done.

'Also, this way won't bring too much attention to Eva, I think, as it's just a piece of paper,' said Sofie, ever practical.

Eva hoped so, already she was getting known as the 'photo-girl', she didn't want that information to get into the wrong hands.

\*

When she fell asleep, she dreamt of Michal. It felt so real, his head was shaved, his green eyes were dull and dark, there were bruises under his eyes, and his cheekbones stood out starkly in his pale face.

He was working outside in the snow, standing in line with several other men, all laying down bricks. He hadn't seen her, and she started to walk fast to try to get to him. Her shoes were slipping in the mud, which turned suddenly to heavy banks of snow. She struggled to get through, shouting his name, till she was hoarse, but no sound came out of her mouth, and he never looked up, and the more she tried the further he seemed to get.

She woke with a start, the scream dying on her lips, her heart hammering against her chest. She sat up coughing and wheezing, feeling weak and tired.

During the morning *Appell*, Hinterschloss was being particularly vile. Eva could smell the alcohol a metre away before he

112

stopped in front of her, a sneer on his face, his yellow eyes seeming to glow. 'Kanada, eh, you're ready for that today?'

She nodded.

'Can you not use your mouth? Answer me!'

He shoved her with the end of his rifle and her knees buckled. There would be thick welts there later.

'Yes, sir,' she said quickly, straightening fast.

'Weren't you just in the hospital?'

She blanched. Meier must have told him. She had been right then to trust her instincts, and not to reveal too much to him through Sofie. Though she supposed Hinterschloss must have wondered where she'd been too. All of this and more raced through her fear-heightened brain.

'Yes. I was, briefly.'

'Are you ill still?' he asked, his glazed eyes penetrating as he stepped forward, touching her forehead. She had to bite her cheek to stop herself from shoving his hand away. He made a show of wiping his hand on his trousers, a look of disgust on his face.

'No,' she shook her head, 'not anymore, it was some time ago.'

'Not that long.'

Eva didn't know how exactly she'd been lucky enough to escape his notice till then about her illness, perhaps he was just in a particularly foul mood now and was looking for a reason to pick on someone even if it was for something from a while back.

She was still very weak, her limbs felt heavy and she was easily tired. With the right nutrition and rest, recovery would have been possible, but here with neither available – not to mention the unsanitary surroundings – it was likely to be a long road to recovery.

'So, you are strong?'

'Yes,' she lied.

He quirked a brow. 'How strong?'

She hoped he wouldn't make her lift another rock above her head for hours, she didn't know if she had it in her, to be honest.

'I am capable of work – I can carry on at the Kanada, sir.'

He looked surprised, and even laughed, slapping a knee in his sudden mirth. 'Oh ho! What's this, what's this!' he said to one of the *Kapos* who also began to laugh.

'Silly girl,' she said.

Hinterschloss seemed to approve as his yellow eyes lit up. Then he looked at Eva, 'Yes, *very* silly. So because you were ill you think you deserve special treatment – to get one of the better assignments here, is that it?'

Eva swallowed. 'No, I didn't mean that.'

'You didn't?' he sneered. Poking a finger into her chest, hard, so that it hurt, making her gasp. 'So, you get ill and the others must carry on working hard outside in all-weathers while you get a cushy post?'

He bared his sharp teeth in a leer.

'No.'

'No?' His grey eyes flared.

'No, I mean I don't need special treatment, sir, I can work anywhere.'

There was a long silence. Then one of the other guards called out something about needing to get a move on, and he sniffed as if the man had ruined his fun, then looked back at her.

'Anywhere, eh? Fine, you can join the construction team, they need someone to break up the rocks.' Then he smirked. 'I seem to recall that you have experience with those.'

She opened and closed her mouth.

His hand moved towards his rifle. 'Is this a problem?'

'No, sir.'

'Good – go, you've delayed us all already, there won't be a next time.'

Her hands felt the tiny portrait hidden against her ribs – how would she get a chance to give it to Herman now?

Spring was supposed to be on its way, but instead snow was falling in heavy drifts. She wrapped the thin scarf she'd managed to get in the warehouse around her head and shuffled forward to join the crew who would begin the twelve-hour shift of breaking up rocks, in the freezing cold.

That night, before the curfew as she walked outside with her hands swollen into claws from the icy weather, red and painful, she gave Sofie the portrait of Michal. 'Can you give it to Herman, if you see him?'

Sofie looked at her and then wrapped her scarf over Eva's hands in an attempt to warm them.

'I'll try. It might take some time. He doesn't clean in the hospital anymore, but sometimes I have to go to the storerooms for supplies, and it goes past the fence where he is working now.'

'Thanks, whenever you can.'

Vanda and Helga and several other women from the Kanada were moved to the same work unit a week later, and joined Eva in a new barrack that was reserved mostly for labour units. The new accommodation was far more crowded. Still, Sofie managed, with a bit of bribery on the part of Meier, to move into Eva's new barrack too. Their new *Kapo* was a Polish woman by the name of Maria, who seemed the kind to look the other way if the price was right. It took a month before Sofie got the chance to go past the fence and find Herman.

She coughed, then dropping it at his feet, she motioned to the ground, and he stealthily pocketed it.

'And now we wait,' said Sofie that night, 'and see.'

Eva nodded.

Her hands were split and painful. She was tired and starving. There were no extra rations or scraps to be had – it was difficult to find anything to barter with when you were working outdoors, it wasn't like when she was in the Kanada where there was always something she could trade for extra food.

She'd got painfully thin, and there were sores on her legs that weren't healing properly.

'Here,' said Sofie, giving her a thick wedge of black bread, bigger than their usual evening ration.

'No, Sofie,' she protested, 'I won't take your food.'

'You have to, Eva, or you're not going to make it, not on these rations. You're already too thin. Besides, I'm working in a hospital, we get extra food sometimes.'

'You're lying,' Eva said, eyes narrowing. She stared at her friend, and wondered – had she slept with Meier so that she could get this? She didn't want to be the reason her friend put herself in danger.

'I'm not,' Sofie said, breaking off a piece of the bread in Eva's hands, and then putting it in her friend's mouth. 'Eat,' she commanded, her dark eyes stern, and Eva began to chew, fighting the urge to shovel the whole thing in her mouth as her hunger pangs gnawed at her.

'I got this through a friend, a nurse from work,' Sofie lied, giving Eva a wedge of cheese afterwards, and then she took out a thick piece of sausage from her headscarf, which she shared with all her bunkmates to their amazed delight.

There was a low gasp. 'Is that real? Or have my eyes just played a trick on me?' whispered Helga, sitting up.

'It's real,' said Sofie with a soft smile.

Vanda scoffed, her eyes narrowing. 'She's lying. She got it from that puppy-eyed guard, Meier. They couldn't stay away from each other, even though she's no longer in the Kanada. I saw them when I passed by the back of the hospital the other day. He couldn't keep his hands off her; he didn't seem to care who saw.'

Sofie looked thunderous but she didn't say anything to deny it. It was true, she'd got away from him for a while, and had been very busy in the hospital. Things had got better for her as a result; Hinterschloss seemed to have found someone else to torment for a while, too, but with her friend still so ill, when Meier had made the pretence of coming past a few days before, she'd told him that she'd missed him.

'You have?' he'd said, surprised, pleased. He looked over his shoulder, and took her hand. They were alone, apart from a few sick patients lying in beds, who had other concerns.

She'd nodded, and he frowned, looked at the floor. 'Every time I've come past you've been too busy… always in a hurry. I thought maybe you didn't want to be my girl anymore.'

Sofie had swallowed, 'No, that's not it. I suppose I'm just distracted… I've been so hungry, it's been a bit hard.'

He'd looked at her. 'You need more food?'

She'd nodded. 'Yes, I think that would make a big difference.'

He'd stared at her for some time. Then he'd given her a small smile, and nodded. 'I understand. I can get you some.'

'You can?' she'd asked.

He touched her arm, and surreptitiously skimmed his hands over her breasts. 'It's a risk, though – if I'm caught. I have to know you are serious about me, about us.'

'I am,' she'd said, fighting the urge to prise his fingers off her thin chest. Then she'd kissed him, and he'd taken her by the hand and pulled her into the shadows so he could kiss her properly, his hands roaming to places he hadn't touched before. She let him. For now she was grateful that he was satisfied with that.

She and Eva had to live, and they wouldn't without food – it was that simple – and as genial as Meier appeared he wouldn't remain so for long until she gave him something more in return. Thankfully he was something of a romantic, and perhaps he liked the idea of the chase.

'It's good of you to share,' said Helga, with a shrug. She wasn't blind to the realities of this place. When one of the women had died in the night a few weeks before, she'd been the first to take the dead woman's shoes and jacket. It was indescribably horrible, yes, but the dead didn't need to be warm, and morals didn't keep food in your belly.

Vanda huffed. 'It's the least she could do after spreading her legs.'

Eva slapped her in the face, hard. The sound rang, making them all flinch in shock. There were white lines imprinted on Vanda's suddenly red face.

Vanda stared at her in shock and gasped, cupping her smarting cheek. 'You bitch, why did you do that?'

Eva's eyes glittered dangerously. 'Because you have no idea what you're talking about.' She had seen the risks that her friend had undertaken and she could guess why she'd gone to speak to Meier now – and the danger it put her in from Hinterschloss who seemed to enjoy terrorising her because of Meier's interest. Sofie denied that Hinterschloss had taken it further, she worried that the more Eva knew the more dangerous it was for them both.

'Leave it, *Kritzelei*.'

Eva shook her head, then glared at Vanda. 'Who are we to judge?'

There was an uncomfortable silence. Vanda touched her reddening cheek, and carried on eating her sausage with tears in her eyes.

After a minute, her eyes softened, and she picked up Sofie's hand and gave it a squeeze. 'I'm sorry,' she said. She wiped her eyes, and sniffed, looking up at her. 'I would probably do it to too, given the chance, if I could make sure my friends could eat.'

'Exactly,' said Eva, taking both their hands. 'We all would.'

'Speak for yourself,' joked Helga. 'I'd only give it up for chocolate.'

The *Kapo* had to tell them to stop laughing.

'Stupid birds,' she muttered.

# FIFTEEN

'You're humming,' said Vanda, who had been assigned the same task as her. Eva swung a hammer to break up a large rock, ignoring the dull ache of pain from the repeated action, as well as the grumble of hunger that was her constant companion. She looked up, wiping a bead of sweat from her eyes. It was cold, and the wind was icy but her cheeks were reddened from being outside all day.

'Was I?' she asked, surprised. Her thoughts, as usual were in the past.

Vanda nodded, and she whistled the tune back in response. 'I know that, I think – Debussy? Or Mozart perhaps?'

Eva paused, her expression soft as she shook her head, in surprise. She hadn't even been aware of what she'd been humming, as she kept time with the hammer. 'No, none of them.'

'I'm sure I know it though – what is it?'

There was a light in Eva's eyes that hadn't been there before. 'I don't think so – it was never released.'

In the distance, there was a shout from one of the guards and they were told to get back to work.

As Eva swung the hammer again, ignoring the way it reverberated against her bare, red and swollen fingers, she slipped back into the memory.

Vanda couldn't have heard it before, because it had only ever been played once in public as far as she knew, and for an audience of one.

*

*Eva woke to the haunting sound of a violin. She sat up in her small bedroom, which overlooked the Wenceslas Square. Prague was fast asleep – the first blush of dawn filtering through the curtains she had left open the night before. As she lay in bed she wondered for a moment if she was still dreaming. But the music played on. She stood up to look out the window, and saw down below, on the street, a figure was playing the softest, sweetest melody she'd ever heard. It was mysterious, and left goosebumps on her arms. Haunting, yet uplifting at the same time.*

*By the time the other windows had opened, and people looked outside to see, the violinist had gone, he'd faded into the rising dawn.*

*Eva didn't go back to sleep, just slipped on her robe, and crept out of the apartment and down the stairs. She saw something poking out of their letterbox, a folded piece of paper. She smoothed it out to find that it was sheet music much scribbled, and redrawn. There was a small note attached.*

'I couldn't draw a portrait of you, but I wrote this. It's what you'd sound like if you were put to music.'

*There was a postscript.*

'P.S. How about breakfast?'

*He mentioned a café around the corner that opened at 7.a.m.*

*She grinned. Had he known she would come downstairs? She raced upstairs, taking them two at a time, then got dressed, whirling to pull a comb through her hair, brush her teeth, and dab some apricot-coloured lipstick on her mouth.*

*She left her parents a quick note that she would be gone for breakfast, before they could protest.*

*In the small café around the corner from their apartment, the scent of just baked bread and freshly brewed coffee welcomed her as she opened the door to a tinkling chime. The windows were fogged, and the cold air slipped in from outside. She saw Michal at the back, sitting at a table, his head bent over a notepad, one hand in his curly hair as he scribbled. He looked up as the door opened, then gave a half grin, showing a dimple.*

*She came to stand across from him, her hands clutching the back of a chair nervously for a moment.*

*'Hello, peach-girl,' he said, standing up and pulling out the chair for her, and she sat down, greeting him with a somewhat shy hello. The night before when they'd walked the city, she'd left*

*feeling confident. Now, in the morning, she felt shy, nervous, on the brink of something momentous.*

*His dark green eyes twinkled as he looked at her.*

*'I didn't know if you'd get my message.'*

*'Which one?' she asked. 'The serenade or the note?'*

*He grinned, ran a hand through his hair. 'Either.'*

*'When did you write it?'*

*'The note?' he asked, taking a sip of his coffee, but his mouth missed the lip as his eyes were fixed on her face. He wiped his chin, with a laugh. She realised, touchingly, that he was nervous too, and it endeared him to her all the more.*

*'The music?' she asked, with a smile.*

*'Last night, after I walked you home. I couldn't sleep…'*

*'You've been up all night?'*

*He nodded, flashing her a smile that she couldn't resist returning. 'I'm used to it – it happens to me when I get inspired, like I can't sit still.' Then he looked away for a moment, admitted, 'I couldn't stop thinking of you.'*

*Eva bit her lip. She'd slept fitfully too. She nodded. 'Me neither.'*

*'Oh, he's good,' said Mila, after Eva knocked on her cousin's door, a few hours later, showing her the music, and Michal's note.*

*Her cousin's large blue eyes scanned the sheet. Her hair was set in bouncing curls, and she had red lipstick on her pretty mouth.*

*'Very good.'*

*Eva stared at her cousin, who had been driving the boys wild since they were in kindergarten.*

*'I don't think it was a technique, if that's what you're implying – something he does with all the girls.'*

*Mila raised a blonde brow, and looked at the music sheet, then up at Eva with a soft smile on her lips – something like wonder – and she nodded, looking at it closely. 'No, I don't think so either. It would have been more practised – this is ... something else.'*

*At Eva's smile, she shook her head, and laughed. 'I do believe, cousin, that you are in trouble.'*

*Eva laughed and sat down on her bed, pausing to move a soft rose-coloured pillow as Mila came to sit down next to her.*

*'I think so too.'*

*Her cousin smirked. 'I am going to enjoy this, I think.'*

*Eva hit her with the pillow.*

*As spring gave way to summer, Eva spent her days sketching in the park or down by the river and the old town, with her friends and cousin, and at night there was always a ticket left for her at the opera house, and she would watch Michal play, sitting in the front row, first looking for those old worn shoes.*

*She loved getting to know the serious soul that lived behind those thoughtful green eyes, after the concert was over; walking with him along the river – night-time was their time, and she lived for the moment he would put his jacket over her shoulders when the weather turned crisp, and the scent of his cologne lingered in her senses, or his hand would find hers.*

*He had a way of making her snort with laughter one minute and thinking about philosophy the next. Sometimes they would just sit quietly together, him passing over some article he thought she might like to read, while she sketched.*

*In the weeks that she got to know him she learnt that Michal had grown up of limited means, yet he came from a family that had once been rather wealthy – they had fallen on hard times when his father had passed away during the First World War. His mother had retreated within herself. Prone to intense highs and lows, she had gone to live with her sister in Austria when he turned sixteen. They had since moved to France, on the eve of the Nazi Anschluss, he hoped she would be doing better now.*

*At age twenty-four he was well on his way to becoming one of the most promising players in the orchestra.*

*He was handsome, head-turningly so, and charming, but he wasn't quite aware of it. Old-fashioned in some respects – not daring for more than a few kisses and making sure she was home by curfew most nights, yet liberal in his thoughts and ideals. He earned good money but sent most of it to his mother. Frugal with himself, generous with others.*

*He was a puzzle, one she wouldn't mind spend years getting to know, and for the first time ever she wished she weren't leaving the city for the rest of the summer.*

\*

Every summer Eva's family went away to a house in the mountains on the edge of a small natural lake outside the town of Jívka in the Hradec Králové Region. The red-roofed farmhouse had been bought by Eva's father and her uncle Bedrich after the birth of their children. The brothers took it upon themselves to restore it, with the result that each summer they found themselves some new project to work on. This year it was a gazebo, for outdoor dining. As Eva's mother put it, 'Let them work, or they'll drive the rest of us crazy.'

It was for everyone a refuge. A place to forget about school and industry. For Eva and her cousin, Mila, the exuberance of childhood cannon balls in the lake, mud pies and tree-houses had given way to sunbathing, sketching and languid starfish laps in the shimmering water.

It was a place to forget about the world as the sun turned their limbs brown and bleached the ends of their hair gold. Night-time by the lake, whatever their age, had been for skinny dipping, sharing their hopes and dreams, and building castles in the air. Eva had always thought how wonderful it was that her best friend was also her cousin.

It was here, inspired by her wild surroundings, that Eva had begun the habit of keeping a sketchbook. Action-sketching she called it, by following mountain squirrels as they scurried up the great trees, or sneaking up on otters as they made their way down the Elbe river.

*The house was a remote hideaway, without a telephone and traversed only by a thin, winding dirt path, but despite its out-of-the way locale, the postman had added it to his route, due to the combined charms of Bedrich's legendary card games and their housekeeper Kaja's excellent apple pie.*

*One afternoon, Eva stood in the doorway, her long hair wet from swimming, dripping on the rag-rug welcome mat, causing Kaja to furrow a brow, grab a towel by the console and proceed to attack her hair, while moaning that she'd waxed the floors just that morning. Eva shrugged the fussing woman's hands away, and stepped back onto the rug. Her eyes fixed on the sight of the postman with nervous anticipation, avoiding Kaja's knowing, slightly exasperated smile. Eva had run all the way from the lake when she'd heard his familiar whistle, and saw his shuffling stride. He doffed a flat cap at her, his watery brown eyes softening as he noticed her excited state. He looked at Kaja and said, 'Oh, to be young again.'*

*Kaja snorted. 'Speak for yourself.'*

*Eva danced on the mat, shuffling from foot to foot in anticipa-tion. There was a towel wrapped around her, but she was still in her striped bathing suit, and he gave her an indulgent smile as he handed over a letter. 'It's here, dítě,' he said with a wink. 'From your young man.'*

*Eva coloured, but she couldn't help the wide smile that split across her face as she clutched the letter to her chest. 'Thank you!' she cried, before fleeing down the path towards the lake, Kaja's calls to be careful and not to break her neck drifting off in the* distance – along with something about a warm chocolate babka that had just come out of the oven, and would he like a slice?

Eva raced back to the edge of the small, natural lake to read it in private, but it wasn't to be.

'Is that from Michal?'

Eva whirled around, then seeing her mother, she grinned, nodding.

Eva's mother, Anka, was seated at a long wooden table, a glass of lemonade in her manicured hand, her Dachshund, Chatzy – who had large, sad brown eyes – at her feet. Anka put down her magazine. Her dark, curled hair shone in the sunshine.

Anka Copco, it must be said, did not give up her standards, even for the mountains. And if the men wanted to build things and spend their time being mountaineers she would leave them to it, just so long as they kept it to themselves.

Eva tore the letter open, her eyes scanning Michal's words, written in a slanting, scrawling hand. She sat down on the chair opposite her mother to read, hazel eyes alight.

Eva smiled, as she recounted parts of it aloud. 'They played Don Giovanni last night, a special performance because some celebrity musician attended.' She scanned the rest and then snorted. 'He had to buy a new pair of shoes.'

Her mother laughed too.

She read the part about him missing her to herself.

'I smelt peaches in the market, and for a moment I saw your face, someone told me that I had stopped in the middle of the road without realising.'

*She set the letter down, her stomach doing a flip. Before her family had come to their country house, she'd spent almost every day with him – when they had started getting ready to depart for the old house in the mountains, she'd dragged her feet.*

*As she'd packed, her mother stood at the doorway, a knowing look on her face. 'Your father tells me that you asked if you could stay behind this year, dítě. Has this got something to do with a certain boy who has been keeping my daughter out late every night, ruining her complexion?'*

*Eva straightened, and glanced at herself quickly in mirror, then laughed. There were deep circles beneath her hazel eyes from her late nights waiting for Michal to finish at the symphony and their long walks through the city. It was a magic time that felt made just for the two of them. And as the long hours of daylight stretched through summer, they would watch the sunset together before he walked her home.*

*She grinned, 'What does uncle Bedrich say – "sleep when you're dead"? I haven't wanted to miss anything this summer.'*

*Her mother smiled. 'Bedrich takes a nap every single day at two!' she scoffed. 'It is wonderful to see you so happy, though, dítě. But a few weeks in the country will be good for you too.'*

*It had been good. The mountains were as beautiful as they ever had been, her cousin's laughter just as infectious. But it felt as if a part of her had been left behind in Prague.*

*She shook her head at herself, and laughed now, leaning against her mother. 'You know, I used to tease Mila about stuff like this, pining over some boy.'*

*Her mother's arm came around her shoulders, playing with her wet hair. There was a soft smile on her red lips. 'Well, her head was always turned by some young man, she was always a little bit in love. You, well, you never did give your heart to anything lightly, not art, your family, your friends – you always give it your all.'*

*This was true. Even as children, Mila had had a crush on almost every boy in the class. By the time they were nine she had married them all in the playground, and caused a few of her 'husbands' to get into some rather raucous fights.*

*The sound of laughter carried on in the distance. Eva and Anka looked up to see Mila running from the lake in a red bathing costume, Arnold hot on her heels in shorts, his strong muscular thighs making short work of the distance as he scooped her up over his shoulder and proceeded to march her back to the lake where he threatened to toss her in.*

*Mila had met Arnold – a lawyer with a boyish laugh, and kind eyes – the previous summer. He hadn't been impressed by Mila's coquettish ways, and had put her in her place rather quickly when she'd tried dating him and someone else at the same time. When he walked away, declaring that he deserved better, to everyone's surprise, she'd agreed, and she'd sent him roses to apologise. By then she was head over heels in love.*

*It had been a whirlwind romance.*

*'Cousin! Eva, come save me!' cried Mila, her long blonde hair a tumble of curls over his shoulder, her eyes dancing as she shrieked.*

*Mila and Arno were getting married in the spring — she'd finally found the boy who'd catch her. Eva laughed. Then set the letter down to save her cousin.*

\*

*It was late afternoon, and the lake was ablaze, the water shimmering in golden light. Eva's sketchbook lay abandoned, just fallen out of her hand onto the grass, as she dozed.*

*She stretched her legs on a big stripy towel. The neighbour's cat, Scarecrow, a fluffy straw-coloured thing with a squashed face and a grumpy temperament to match, nestled into the crook of her arm, and she gave in to the temptation for a nap with him.*

*A shadow fell across her face, and she squinted, a hand cupping her eyes, only for her to blink and sit up fast, prompting the cat to make a disapproving sound as he skittered away somewhere he wouldn't be disturbed.*

*Eva squinted, and then she saw him.*

*His face was bathed in gold, which turned the edges of his curls a soft honeyed brown, and his laughing green eyes were crinkled at the corners.*

*'You're here,' she breathed.*

*His mouth formed a soft smile, as he stared down at her. 'I couldn't stay in Prague.'*

*She'd stared, marvelling at the sight of him, here with her. 'Why not?'*

*'Because you weren't there.' Then he kissed her.*

# SIXTEEN

Sofie was tired, there were deep circles beneath her eyes. She'd heard about a woman who matched Lotte's description, but it had turned out to be another dead end, and she was beginning to wonder if she would ever find her, or if the letter from her cousin's neighbour, which had led her here, to hell, was simply a wild and foolish goose chase. She sat on the edge of the bunk, her eyes glazed, not seeing as a pair of women squabbled over stolen shoes. She was lost in time, to the moment when everything had changed.

*

*She was standing in the front of the shop, watching Tomas who was smiling as he crawled towards her. He gave her that impish grin that was always hard to resist.*

*The shop bell chimed, and the sound of heavy jackboots were loud on the wooden floors.*

*Sofie looked from her son to see two men with hard eyes and amused sneers entering the building.*

*'Can I help you?' she asked, as Tomas began to crawl towards them, his little fist coming forward to shake on a trouser leg.*

*It happened before she could blink, before she could even snatch him away.*

*The man reacted fast, shoving him aside. His hooded blue eyes flared. 'Take your dirty fingers off me.'*

*Sofie raced forward to pick up her child, who had toppled over, and begun to wail in loud, piercing shrieks. 'You monster! How dare you – you have no right to touch him!' she cried, picking up her baby and trying to soothe him while she glared at the intruders. 'Get out of our shop!' she commanded.*

*He simply sneered, 'I'm here to hand out the orders – and actually I have every right to be here. It's you who no longer has any,' he spat.*

*She blinked, she'd known this boy, not well, but his father had been in to the shop before. He was small of stature, scrawny, and there were spots on his chin.*

*From his workshop in the back, she could hear her father's voice calling out, 'What is it, Sofie, what's going on?' as he hurried inside to where the commotion had centred.*

*'Just a warning,' said the boy with hooded eyes. 'For now,' he added, sharing a sly look with his partner.*

*He handed them a notice, which he was careful not to place directly in her father's hands, but on the glass counter.*

*Then he turned and left, giving Sofie one last lingering look of warning from his hooded eyes before he did.*

*Her father picked up the piece of paper, and read the notice with a frown. His eyes widened in disbelief. 'It says that from now on it is illegal for a Jew to own a business.'*

He staggered to the armchair nearby, and sat down with a thud.

'Illegal?' Sofie repeated, dumbstruck. Her large, dark eyes stared at him, trying to make sense of his words. 'But it's been in the family for more than a century!'

Her father looked up at her, looking suddenly younger than his years. 'What are we going to do?'

*

They decided to put the business in a friend's name, a gentile. It was her grandfather's idea, and it was a good one, or at least so they thought. But the Nazis saw through it.

In the night, while she'd been putting away some stock, the glass rained down from above, landing on Sofie's head, and she fell backwards crashing into a wall of shelves. They upended, and hundreds of watch faces fell, breaking into shattered pieces on the hardwood floor. Sofie lay in a pool of her own blood. Her ears rang, and it was hard to see or hear beyond the slick of her blood.

Distantly, there was worry, and in the quiet before the hum of noise began again, her first and only thought was for her son, Tomas.

'Tomas!' she called. Her voice was weak, then grew louder, her gaze blurring, her ears ringing all the more. Her head pounded. She put a hand to her temple and it came back wet with blood. She blinked. What had happened?

Suddenly there were footsteps, hard hob-nailed boots, and all she saw was brown – brown uniformed legs. Nazis, she realised with a shiver of fear, thugs.

*She sat up, cradling her head and calling for her son. She could hear him, somewhere, crying out, calling for her.*

*She crawled forward, blinking, then suddenly there was a voice, and a face that smelt like old whisky and rage, hot and rancid. Cold, hooded blue eyes seared her flesh. Her hair was snatched back by a hard hand, and he hissed as her head snapped towards his. 'I told you, you should have just left.' Then he slammed a fist in her face, and she fell back on a jagged piece of glass. She knew nothing after that.*

\*

Hours later Sofie woke with a headache. It felt as if her head was splitting in two.

She was on the sofa, and her father was sitting next to her, his greying head in his hands.

'Udo can get us out, he says he knows a way,' he said, as soon as her eyes were open. She blinked, staring up at him. It looked like he'd aged twenty years overnight from all that had happened in the space of a few weeks. Their shop ambushed, their citizenship stripped away. All because they'd happened to do nothing more offensive than exist. 'He knows someone who can get us through to Switzerland by boat. We'll have to leave tonight.'

Sofie made to get up, her head pounding from the sudden movement. She flinched at the pain, but pushed through. 'I'll pack our things, get Tomas ready.'

He shook his head. 'Already done. Your grandparents will follow us in a few days, we must go now.'

*She nodded. 'Yes.'*

\*

*They travelled by train for several hours. Her father's friend, a local businessman, had helped to arrange the papers to get them out. On the first stop the guard checked them over, and Sofie held her breath. It was illegal for Jews to travel more than a few kilometres from their homes, leave the country or travel in anything but the third-class carriages. She wore a woollen hat low over her forehead, but the bandage still showed. He frowned, then asked how she'd got it. She looked at Tomas, mercifully asleep in his cot, and said, 'Tripping over my son, you know how it can be – I wasn't looking.'*

*The guard pulled a face and her father added, 'Mother's instinct to save her son, she went flying down the stairs instead. Women,' he muttered with a wink.*

*The guard laughed. 'Yes, silly things,' he said, then handed her back her papers. 'Be careful now.'*

*'I will,' she said, too afraid to be offended.*

\*

*That evening they arrived at the station in Bregenz, at the foothills of the Alps, where they were met by her cousin, Lotte and her husband, Udo. The pair had looked after her when she'd given birth to Tomas. 'The boat will get you through to Switzerland,' Udo explained, running a hand through coarse black hair, his dark eyes solemn. 'You can use my car – we'll follow in a few days to avoid suspicion.'*

They nodded. Lotte rubbed her throat in anxiety. She was a motherly sort, plump with short blonde hair and a permanently worried expression. She had big, round doe eyes, that looked terrified at everything that was happening. She didn't say much, just twisted her fingers together so much that she had caused the skin to bleed.

Sofie and her father didn't comment. They were tired, hungry and miserable too. Sofie understood how her cousin felt, she wouldn't feel safe until she was properly out of the country, but it was enough to at least be out of Vienna, and away from all that had happened.

After a light dinner, they went to bed, hoping that tomorrow they would find themselves a new home. 'Maybe we should rethink this,' Lotte said again. 'Try something else. This is just so risky.'

Sofie sighed. Her cousin had said it a few times already, and they'd grown impatient in explaining that this was their only chance. It was either leave or wait for them to come find them.

Udo pinched the bridge of his nose. 'Enough, Lotte. This is the only way.'

Sofie escaped from their bickering, knowing it was just the fear talking. She held her son close, breathed in his fresh scent after his bath, and whispered. 'I'll make sure you don't have to grow up with this fear, somehow. I promise you. I won't let anyone tell you that you're a second-class citizen again.'

*

*They were hurrying towards the lake and the small waiting boat that would lead them to Switzerland, and freedom, when suddenly there were shouts from behind them, and several SS officers raced towards them, calling the attention of the border patrol guard who had waved them through moments before, and hadn't asked too many questions. As she cradled Tomas, Sofie could see her cousin being dragged forward by two Nazis, howling. 'I'm so sorry!' Lotte wailed. 'They said they would kill us if we didn't tell them the truth!'*

*Sofie closed her eyes in horror.*

*'They have falsified their papers,' said the officer to the patrol guard.*

*'No,' Sofie denied it. 'They're real.'*

*The officer struck her across the face. Sofie's father shouted, and suddenly he was dragged across the gangway, a gun pointed at his head.*

*'No! Please, don't!' shouted Sofie.*

*The officer looked at her. 'I don't like liars,' he spat. 'Or Jews,' before he shot her father in the heart.*

*'No, Papa!' she screamed. She watched as her father gasped for breath, then died. She fell to her knees, sobbing, clutching her son, who started to wail. Lotte came forward to take him from her, her plump face full of remorse.*

*Sofie snatched him away from her cousin, and an officer picked her up roughly, dragging her away from her father, forcing Tomas from her arms. He handed the baby to Lotte and sneered, 'Take care of this.' Then he looked at Sofie and said, 'You are under arrest for trying to leave on falsified papers.'*

*Lotte started to cry, over Tomas's wails. 'I am so sorry.'*

*Sofie's lips trembled, hot tears splashing from her lashes. 'Look at what you did – what you caused. Was it worth my father's life?'*

*They took her to a nearby police station, where she was kept in a holding cell and told that they would decide what to do with her in time. Sofie sat in the same clothes that she had crossed the border in, and couldn't find it in her to bathe or wash or fix her hair, even though her cousin had brought her suitcase by a few days before.*

*All she wanted was her son. She ached for him, ached for her father. The tears had stopped flowing, perhaps they were drowning her from the inside, suffocating her heart.*

*'What has happened to my son?' she asked the guard, when he came past with a small bowl of soup that she wouldn't be eating. It had been several days and she hadn't heard anything. 'Is he with my cousin?'*

*The guard looked at her. 'Your cousin?'*

*'The woman that sold me out,' she spat.*

*He blinked. 'The blonde Jew? Same thing that will happen to you no doubt – she was sent to a camp.'*

*Sofie stood up fast, blinking in shock. 'And my son?'*

*He picked his teeth idly. 'There was no child when they took her.'*

*'What do you mean?' she screamed.*

*He took a step away from her. 'She was alone. Said she gave the baby up – wouldn't say where. It didn't matter to us.'*

*Sofie felt as if her heart had shattered into a thousand pieces. 'Where is she – which camp?'*

*He shrugged. 'She was sent East.'*

*Sofie sunk to her knees in despair, as the guard left without a backward glance.*

*Falsifying papers was a serious offence, and there were two punishments for such a crime: the first was death by firing squad, the second was to be sent as a prisoner to a labour camp. Not that Sofie was given an option. She was told the following morning that she would be sent to a camp and there they would decide her fate.*

*She was sent out on a crowded train with hundreds of others: men, women and children.*

*The train travelled for several hours, and then ground to a sudden screeching stop.*

*In the close quarters of the cattle cart – which smelt of waste and unwashed bodies – people were staring out of the slats but no one was sure what had happened.*

*Suddenly, the doors opened, and they were pulled off the train, and ushered onto a platform along with another cart, which had been going in another direction. 'Stay here,' they were commanded.*

*She watched in horror as a man was killed just for tripping and getting in a guard's way.*

*After several hours standing around, heart hammering in her chest, Sofie slowly made her way to the other transport, her eyes darting back and forth, amazed that she had managed it. She would give another name, she thought, and perhaps have another fate, she hoped. She needed to live so that she could find Lotte. So that she could find her son.*

*She was right, as the train she'd chosen took her to Westerbork, a transit camp and ghetto. The one she'd been on was bound straight for Mauthausen, the death camp.*

*The smallest thing could make a difference, she realised. Going right instead of left. Life or death based on the smallest bit of luck.*

# SEVENTEEN

'Spring is coming,' said Eva. It was a Sunday, the one day a week where they didn't have to work, where they were free to roam around outside near their blocks. To meet and talk without fear.

Sofie looked at her in surprise. It was freezing. The snow was ankle deep, and her breath came out in puffs of clouds.

'Look,' said Eva, pointing. There in a small drift by her feet was a snowdrop. 'While all this has been happening, underneath, in the ground, spring is on its way.'

Eva knelt down to look at the unexpected beauty of it in a place so desolate and barren as this.

Her back ached from her long hours working outside, which had begun to take a toll on her health. She tortured herself imagining the housekeeper Kaja's warm chocolate *babka*, fresh from the oven. Long summer days by the lake, Michal's eyes, her mother's soft smile.

'Slow-cooked beef goulash,' said Sofie, carrying on an earlier conversation. 'That's what I'd have for lunch today if it were Sunday, not the prime cuts, but it wouldn't matter, if you cooked it long enough. I'd be at my grandparents' home, the flat would be warm, cosy. Tomas would be asleep in his crib, fresh from his bath or playing on the floor with the dog. My father would be doing the crossword, and I would have made bread – the way my grandmother had shown me as a child.'

She looked at Eva, her eyes sad. 'That's what I would be doing now, instead of this.'

Eva nodded, touched her arm. She didn't know sometimes if it was better to let their old lives go or not, but it helped to remember them anyway, to be more than the animals they tried to reduce them to.

'Would there be potatoes in the stew?' she asked.

Sofie smiled. 'A mountain of them. My grandmother grew them in her tiny garden in pots, buttery soft, crumbling into your mouth, tasting of tomato and paprika.'

'Mmmmh,' said Eva, picturing the taste, mouth-watering.

'I'll tell you one thing,' said Sofie. 'If I ever make it out of this place alive, I won't be eating watery soup ever again.'

Eva nodded. 'Or black bread.'

'If we ever get out of this, I'll teach you how to make bread, we'll have tea and knead dough, and outside it won't matter if the sky is falling as we'll be warm and dry with full bellies.'

Eva looked at her and smiled, eyes softening. They both knew that was unlikely, but it made them feel better to think of it, to have hope that maybe one day they could live in that world again.

\*

A week later, and spring seemed like a distant dream. An icy wind had rattled through the camp, and no one spoke of the change in season any more.

Sofie fell behind the others. Eva had gone ahead to speak to a woman she used to know that lived in her neighbourhood, and the two women shared food, and stories. On Sundays, smiles came a little quicker, and feet shuffled somewhat easier.

Sofie's though were leaden. She'd done her usual routine, spent the morning asking everyone she met for news of Lotte. It was the same thing she did every Sunday, the same thing she would continue to do, except after five months in Auschwitz, she was beginning to lose hope.

Eva came back to her side, handing her a small piece of cheese that she'd managed to trade with one of the other women. Sofie took it but didn't eat.

'Are you all right?' asked Eva, concerned, noting her friend's vacant eyes. 'Is it Meier? Has he done something?'

Sofie looked up, past Eva, to where the guard stood near the fence. He was always there. His blue gaze on hers, begging for more.

She shook her head, looked away, her eyes unseeing, past the snaking rows of women walking, some arm in arm, as they ambled outside in the cold wintry light. Suddenly, she straightened. The precious wedge of cheese fell out of her fingers to the ground, in her shock.

'What is it?' asked Eva.

Sofie didn't say a word. Her mouth seemed to open involuntarily and close. Her gaze clamped on a cluster of women who were walking past their block. They were older, and one had a patch of bright blonde hair.

Sofie blinked. Then grabbed Eva's hand. 'It's her – it's Lotte.'

'Are you sure?' breathed Eva, staring across the expanse of churned-up mud to the women walking past.

But Sofie had raced off before replying, Eva in hot pursuit.

# EIGHTEEN

*Prague, Autumn 1938*

'Married? Are you mad, Eva? You have only just met this boy. Though I see you have been out with him every night this week,' her father said, putting his morning newspaper down. There was a frown between his eyes.

Eva's eyes danced, ignoring his protestations.

'Still, Papa. We will be getting married. I just thought you should know.'

Eva's mother laughed, waving a manicured hand as she poured coffee from the carafe on the impeccably laid breakfast table into a fine blue china mug. Outside, the city of Prague was bathed in morning light, and Wenceslas Square below was a riot of autumn colour. Anka's dark eyes were amused. 'She's not serious, she's just teasing you, Otto.'

'I am not,' said Eva. She poured herself some apple juice, and gave them a stern look. 'It is a fact, that will come true in time. I can carry on at art college when we are married – so there will be no interruption to my studies, or my desire to have a job in illustration or textile design, I still haven't made up my mind on that just yet –

*thankfully, he is not one of those men who don't want their wives to have lives, unlike Mila's Arnold, though, as you know, Mila is happy to be traditional so long as she can host all the parties,' she said with a fond grin, '… speaking of that, I'm sure babies can wait for a few years while we get our lives settled. We'll probably live in his small apartment which isn't far from here so we could still do Shabbat easily with the family, not that we do it that often. Anyway, he will be busy in the day, with his music, so I can come and see you often, as usual. Maybe in a year or two we will start a family though…' she babbled, painting her vision of the future for them.*

*Her father's eyes bulged in shock as he choked on his coffee, which he spat up over the crisp linen tablecloth. He picked up a napkin and wiped his mouth. 'That is ridiculous. I have only met this man a few times, for goodness' sake – the first didn't create the best impression either, when he arrived, as I remind you, unannounced and uninvited I might add, to our private summer house.'*

*'Oh, Papa, he didn't even stay the night, even though Mother offered. He just came to say hello because he missed me, surely that's not a crime,' said Eva with a grin.*

*'He made the journey just for that – exactly my point!'*

*'Mine too!' agreed Eva, meaning something quite different to her father. To her it conveyed what kind of a person Michal was – the kind who wasn't afraid to show someone how much they meant to them, no matter the cost to himself.*

*'I wish he had stayed,' said Anka. 'We had room, besides,' she said rather wickedly, her slanted eyes shining, 'he does add a*

certain something when he's around, don't you think, Eva – like that interesting shade to your father's complexion?'

Her father frowned, glaring at his wife, not about to be teased over such a serious matter. 'It was not a question of room,' he said, ignoring her other jibe completely. Not that Michal had asked to stay, he'd stayed only for the evening, he wouldn't hear of imposing. They'd gone swimming and by the time he'd left she'd known that what she was feeling wasn't some schoolgirl crush – it was real love, perhaps for the first time in her life.

'It's a question of who he is and whether he would be a good match,' continued her father, not noticing his daughter's distracted gaze, as she stared off into the distance, thinking about how she would decorate the tiny apartment. Bijou, she thought, correcting herself. French-inspired perhaps. Lots of colour... 'Marriage is not something to be taken lightly, dítě.'

Eva's attention snapped back to him as her father stressed, 'He has hardly any family, how can we know if he's a good man or not? I cannot allow this, he hasn't even had the decency to ask my permission to marry you himself!'

He rested his hands together as if his words had provided an end to the discussion.

Eva sighed, waving a hand in the air to scrub away all her father's concerns. 'He is a good man, in fact he is a wonderful person. You know, Papa, people show you who they are when they think you are not looking. When they think no one is watching. And you know what Michal does?'

*Despite himself her father blinked and said, 'What?'*

*'He is the sort of person who puts a blade of grass in a stranger's book when the mother is dragged off to the river to look at the boats by her children, so that she won't lose her place. He puts a hand out to stop children from crossing the street before the light changes. He gives every woman young or old his seat.'*

*'These are little things, Eva, they don't mean anything.'*

*'I disagree. It's the little things that make you who you are. Besides, he does have family, they have left the city – because of all the troubles, the fears about what will happen with Germany since the Anschluss.'*

*Her father pursed his lips. 'So why didn't he?'*

*'He didn't want to leave the symphony.'*

*Her father sighed. 'So, he showed more loyalty to his company than his family?'*

*'He didn't want to abandon his country, and why should he have to leave just because of some rumours? We haven't.'*

*Her father shrugged. 'Maybe we should have.'*

*Her eyes widened. 'What do you mean?'*

*'It's just that things are getting worse now. People are worried about the meeting with Hitler and the allies. It's not certain that he won't get the Sudetenland, after all.'*

*'No one will let that happen, I'm sure – after Austria it would be madness to allow him more territory. Besides, you can't hold it against Michal if we haven't left our homes either.'*

Her father conceded that at least. 'I've been listening too much to Bedrich, it's probably all going to be fine. But look, I know you think you are in love with this man—'

'I don't just think it, Papa—'

'Still, I think you should wait. Eva. Wait to know. Marriage isn't a joke,' he said, looking at his wife, who gave him an unamused look.

Eva grinned. 'I don't need to wait, Papa, I know it the way that I know that spring comes early to Prague, that the sun rises in the east, and the way you always smile without realising when you hear the sound of heels, because it could be Mama coming through the door.'

Anka and Otto shared a soft look at that.

Eva continued, 'But I will wait if that's what you want. If you want to get to know him first, to see what I see. But I can tell you right now, he is the man I will marry. If he'll have me.'

'Eva!' gasped her mother, her red-lipsticked lips parting in surprise. 'You mean to tell us he hasn't asked you yet?'

Eva grinned. 'No, not yet anyway. I'm just preparing you.'

Her father stared at her, speechless.

Eva's eyes danced in amusement. 'I haven't asked him yet, if that's what you are worried about.'

He laughed. 'Heaven forbid. Sometimes you are too like your mother.'

She looked at Anka. She was the most indomitable person she knew, she'd proposed to the man she loved too – it's why she was here in this world. 'Isn't that a good thing?'

*He smiled. 'Of course. But why don't you at least wait until he asks you, before we start picking out your trousseau, all right?'*

*She snorted. 'I don't see why. He might take far too long. This is a person who has spent fifteen years composing the same piece of music. I think he is not the sort of person who rushes things. He told me just yesterday that despite the fact that he recently bought new shoes, he still thinks the old shoes he always wears have got a few more good years left. You must see them, they are very old.'*

*Her father's lips twitched. 'I'm beginning to like him more and more.'*

*Eva laughed. 'I'll give him till the end of the year, all right? Then, I'll ask him myself.'*

*'I suppose that will do,' said her father, giving her mother a helpless look.*

*In the end she hadn't needed to – in the autumn, as they had feared, Sudetenland had been incorporated into the German empire, and many were saying that the rest of Czechoslovakia might soon be under occupation.*

*'It's a terrible time to ask,' Michal said, taking her hand as they sat in her parents' living room, after they'd listened in horror to the news on the radio. He looked at Eva's father, then at Eva. 'I would like to ask your permission to marry your daughter, if she will have me.'*

*Eva was the only one who found the will to make a joke that it had taken him long enough.*

*By then, Michal was an accepted part of their lives, and in the few short weeks since Eva had told her parents her intentions, they had seen what kind of a man he was, and how much he adored their daughter.*

*Her father nodded, then came forward to embrace him. 'We need good news on a day like this.'*

*'But, Otto, shouldn't we do something now?' asked Anka. 'Bedrich has ideas, he has been saying that we should leave, that we might come under occupation. I mean, if the rumours of what they have done to the Jews in Austria is anything to go by... surely they will bring this trouble here?' Her eyes were wide, fearful.*

*'This isn't Austria. He won't be able to get away with that here.' He shook his head. 'Bedrich is panicking, it won't come to that.'*

Sofie pushed past a sea of women towards the plump woman. 'Lotte!' she cried.

She didn't turn, or stop, as they began to walk away.

Sofie ran forward, her lungs on fire from the short amount of exercise she had done on her weak, malnourished legs. She grabbed the woman's arm, roughly, shouting, 'Lotte! Stop!'

The woman paused and looked at her, wrenching her arm out of her grip. 'What do you want?'

Sofie blinked, then felt as if she'd been plunged in ice. Hot, choking tears threatened to fall.

*It wasn't her.*

She swallowed and the woman stared at her, with big green eyes. Sofie dashed away a tear, angrily. 'I – I'm sorry I thought you were my cousin, Lotte—' She closed her eyes, and her legs started to shake and she was about to collapse. 'You look just like her, except for the eyes.'

Eva dashed forward to catch her, holding her close. She had heard the exchange, and her heart ached for her friend.

'I'm sorry,' said Sofie, and she nudged Eva so the two could leave. Not-Lotte's hand came out to stop her. 'Very similar, you say?'

Sofie nodded, then looked back at her. 'Yes.'

The woman snorted. 'I think I know her.' She looked at the others – whose eyes widened. 'One of the stupid guards thought I was someone else, asked me why I was not in my usual barracks, why I had been moved, had to recheck the numbers,' she said, referring to her tattoo.

Sofie opened and closed her mouth. 'Do you know which one?'

She pointed towards the end of the row of women's barracks in the distance. 'The last one, there.'

It was getting late and curfew was in place. They were led back to their barracks, and would have to stay there for the night. Sofie waited till the others were asleep, then she snuck out past the *Kapo*'s room on tiptoe. She had found a bucket with a forgotten potato outside the *Kapo*'s room, which she broke in two and put in her brassiere, hardly believing her luck, it would come in handy tonight. If she was caught out of bed, she'd just go to the latrine. Maria didn't police them as heavily as the other *Kapos*, she was lazy, and far more interested in sleeping. She didn't worry about the potato, if she hadn't taken it any one of the hundred women in the barracks would have – it was more likely that their *Kapo* had forgot about it, else she would never have left it. The guards didn't patrol the blocks at night, but there were floodlights and if she was caught, she could get shot. But she had to know. She kept to the shadows as much as possible, stopping to hide near a doorway when she heard the sounds of footsteps, and she waited with her heart beating loudly in her ears for them to die down. It took forty-five minutes but she entered the last barrack of the women's quarters, keeping as quiet as she could. She would sneak into a bunk if the *Kapo* came past, she decided. They were easy to recognise by their armbands, better clothing, and their air of authority.

Sofie peered at the bottom row of bunks. There were hundreds of women.

She approached one, shaking her arm. She whispered, 'Do you know Lotte?' The woman ignored her, and Sofie moved on. She spied one who was sitting up. She asked her too, the woman frowned and looked ready to cry out. Sofie quickly handed her half a potato. The woman stared at it in amazement, then quickly bit into the starchy flesh, her eyes closing in pleasure.

'Lotte?' whispered the woman after some time. 'Blonde woman? Big eyes, plump? Sort of silly?'

Sofie nodded fast. 'Yes, you know her?'

There was a pause and Sofie handed over the other half of the potato. The woman nodded. 'I did.'

Sofie's knees felt like they were about to give way before the woman's words confirmed her deepest fear. 'They killed her last week, she was sick, and they took her away with the others. Gassed.'

Sofie was caught by the *Blockalteste* – the senior officer – who was in charge of their barracks. She was a tall woman named Geneva with dark hair and black slanted eyes. She had been a gynaecologist in Prague, one of the first female doctors. An educated, accomplished woman before she'd been brought here, forced to work at the hospital and perform the sorts of horrible tasks she had never imagined for herself when she had been at medical school. People like Geneva with special skills, even though she was a Jew, had protected status in the camps.

Sofie had only spoken to her once before, she wasn't all that sure if she could trust her or not. 'What are you doing out of bed?' she asked, her eyes suspicious. She was not the sort of woman who would easily be fooled.

Sofie swallowed. She was devastated at what she'd found out. With Lotte's death, she felt as if her best chance of finding out where her cousin had taken her son had died too. Still, there was a part of her that knew she couldn't give up just yet. That Eva had been right – she could still make it out of this place alive, somehow, and search Lotte's neighbourhood – knock on doors, speak to orphanages, someone would have to know *something*, and for that she had to stay alive, keep her wits about her.

'I was at the hospital,' she lied.

Geneva looked at her for a minute, eyes narrowing slightly, and Sofie swallowed.

'And yet you came here to a different barrack afterwards?'

Sofie kept quiet, her brain whirring as she tried and failed to find a good enough excuse for being in the wrong barrack.

'Come with me,' said Geneva, and Sofie's heart started to thud in fear.

Sofie followed her on leaden feet to a private room at the back. It was neat and clean, and there was even a small kitchen area. 'I've seen you working at the hospital,' Geneva noted.

Sofie nodded. 'I'm a nurse.'

The woman's eyes were appraising, she made a *moue* with her lips as she considered her. There was a long silence and the blood started to rush behind Sofie's ears.

'No, you're not.'

Sofie blanched. 'W-why do you say that?'

Geneva considered her. 'The simple things give you away – the way you make a bed, no nurse would do it the way you do. I noticed too that you always seemed to volunteer for the cleaning tasks – anything that won't give you away. Soon, someone will notice.'

It wasn't a threat, Sofie realised, just a statement of fact. A warning, perhaps.

It was true. She'd been doing that now for weeks. There had been a few close shaves, like when she hadn't known how long to sterilise a pair of scissors or the correct way to bandage a leg, but as the doctors didn't perform rounds, this had mostly only been observed by the other nurses – so far no one had tried to turn her in, and one of the others had shown her how to do the task properly, keeping her secret, rather than risking her life.

Sofie swallowed. 'Are you going to tell?' she asked.

Geneva didn't answer and the silence seemed to stretch forever. After a while she said, 'I think I have another idea. You might have to prove something to me first, all right?'

Sofie swallowed. 'Like what?'

'Like, contrary to what I've seen – that you can be trusted.'

Sofie blinked. 'With what?'

Geneva didn't answer her. She frowned, then said, 'Would you like a cup of tea?'

Sofie blinked. 'Tea?'

'Yes.'

'Okay,' she answered.

Seemingly out of nowhere, the *Blockalteste* said, 'I was pregnant when I came here, did you know that?'

Sofie shook her head.

'One of the other doctors – before Mengele arrived this year – delivered the baby. He said it looked Aryan.'

At Sofie's frown, she explained. 'My husband wasn't Jewish, and the baby took after him. He took him away, he made it sound as if it were a great honour – a credit to my skill, which he said would help abort all these other unwanted Jewish children. Except the irony was that mine would get to live – just with Nazis.'

She took a sip of her tea. 'I'm not sure if death would have been better. Mengele probably would have killed my child.'

It was clear that she despised him. Sofie didn't blame her.

Sofie didn't know what to say, except, 'I'm sorry.'

Geneva shrugged and looked away. 'Just another casualty.' She waved a hand, indicating the rest of the complex. 'One of many, not half as interesting as others.' Then she looked up, her gaze direct. 'So did you find her?'

Sofie frowned, 'Who?'

'The woman who gave your child away – the one you snuck out of your barracks to find?'

Sofie's eyes widened. 'How did you know?'

'Word gets around. Not much more to do here besides talk. The other woman – the one who looks like her told me.'

159

'Oh,' said Sofie, cursing herself for not being more discreet.

'So, did you find her?'

'No, she's dead.'

Geneva shook her head sadly. 'I'm sorry too.'

She seemed to stare at her mug for a long time, then she looked up. 'I won't tell anyone about you – but I need your help with a case – I need someone who can be discreet. Someone who isn't afraid to break some rules – to lie if need be. Can you do that?'

Sofie nodded.

'I need an assistant at the hospital, but there will be other tasks, off the books, women we will care for.'

'You want me – even though you know that I'm not a trained nurse?'

'I can train you – it might just save your life. But I warn you – if you betray me, or tell anyone what we're doing, I will not hesitate to have you killed. Do you understand me?'

'Yes.'

'Good.'

'Now get back to your barracks. And report to me tomorrow at the hospital.'

Sofie nodded, and left, wondering what she'd just agreed to do.

# NINETEEN

Eva had frostbite in two of her toes. Her stockings were sodden from the relentless weather. If it wasn't snow, it was rain and sleet and freezing cold mud.

Her body ached no matter which way she moved and hunger was a constant companion. Rations had been slim to begin with but they had got even more so in recent weeks. Some days if she were too slow to get there in time, she missed the midday meal entirely.

Eva was transporting rocks – her sore, swollen feet making it ever harder as she hobbled on in her clogs – when she heard someone call her name. She looked up in surprise. It was Herman.

She rushed forward, looking over her shoulder, to make sure that no one was watching.

There was. Just the *Kapo*, Maria. She was lazy, and not particularly observant, it was their good fortune to have her overseeing them.

'Herman!' she greeted.

'I didn't know if you were still alive,' he said. His bushy eyebrows rose in surprise to take in the sight of her. 'You look terrible.'

She gave a hoarse laugh. 'Thanks, you look good too.' He was thinner than she remembered from the last time, his face drawn. His eyebrows though were as bushy as ever, and his dark eyes, warm.

He chuckled. Then looked over his shoulder. 'Here,' he said, handing her a thick wedge of black bread. Her eyes widened. 'Eat, take it – I was going to trade it later for extra socks, but you need it more.'

She shoved a piece into her mouth and chewed, stopping when one of her teeth at the back seemed to wriggle. She paused, swallowed and felt it with her finger – made a low gasp when it came away and she dropped it on the floor.

Herman looked horrified. 'They aren't feeding you enough – especially not to do this.'

'No,' she agreed, shoving more food into her mouth and chewing on the other side. She looked at him; he would probably have said something by now, but still she couldn't help but ask.

'Have you heard anything? About Michal?'

He looked behind him as a group of women went past, pretending to be helping with the stones.

'Yes, that's why I came to find you.'

She stopped chewing, her mouth opening.

'And? What did you find out? Is he alive?'

He stared at her, his face giving nothing away, and she waited breathlessly for his reply.

# TWENTY

*Prague, Autumn 1938*

*At home things were getting tense.*

*Eva came inside, to find her father, her always-calm, straight-laced father, having a shouting match with her uncle Bedrich.*

*'What's going on?' she asked, hearing the raised voices in the kitchen, just off the hall. Her mother steered her away.*

*'Come, let's go for a walk, let them have it out alone.'*

*But her uncle, hearing their voices, strode out into the entryway. His hat was still on his head, his dark eyes angry. 'Come and talk sense to your father,' he implored.*

*'Don't bring her into this, Bedrich!' hissed her father, following him out into the hall. Eva could see that his face was red and blotchy, she'd never seen him look so cross.*

*'What's going on?' asked Eva, setting her bag on a chair, next to the photograph of her mother's dog, Chatzy, which Anka had placed there partly as it amused her to see her father's beleaguered expression every time he saw it.*

*'He is being stubborn as usual,' said her uncle. 'Believing in the authorities and what little "power" they pretend to have – but*

look at what has happened with this stupid agreement – they all decided our fate and didn't even invite us to have a say!'

He was speaking of the Munich Agreement, where the heads of Britain and France and Russia had met with Hitler in Munich to discuss Czechoslovakia's fate, and agreed to hand over large swathes of the country under Nazi control.

'But we know about this already,' said Eva. 'It's worrisome, yes, but he'll be satisfied with that and—'

Bedrich scoffed. 'Worrisome is an understatement. And satisfied? A man like that? Never. He has been shown that he can take the hand, of course he will come for the arm too. It's time we got serious as a family and made plans to leave, and the sooner the better – like the Jews who got out of Austria.'

'Leave?' repeated Eva. 'And go where? What are you talking about – abandoning our homes?'

Bedrich stared at her, then shook his head. 'Listen to me, Eva. Things are getting worse for Jews all across Europe, many of them as you know have fled here, thinking they would be far from this maniac and his plans—'

'But that's not happening here,' protested her mother. 'We've heard rumours, of course, of how things have been in Austria and Germany – the animosity towards Jews, of course, but it won't stand here.'

Most of their friends were non-Jews, there was no such anti-Semitism from their friends, colleagues, or the people of Prague.

Bedrich showed them a paper; it was a terrible story of Jews being victimised and attacked in the streets of Austria since the

Anschluss, *as if someone had lit a match and the low-level grumble of anti-Semitism that was sometimes still felt in pockets of Europe was suddenly whipped into a frenzy. 'They said that about Austria too. Look, I have a British friend – we were in the army together – he has a summer home in Sussex and he said we could use it if we needed to restart our lives. I think it's worth considering.'*

*'England,' said Anka, her eyes incredulous. He may as well have said the moon.*

*'Yes, and why not? They are our allies.'*

*'Our allies?' breathed Otto. 'After what they did at that agreement, you think so?'*

*'But it's so far away,' said Anka. 'And only Eva knows the language.'*

*'Not much of it,' said Eva.*

*Bedrich looked hen-pecked. 'Do you have a better option, Otto?'*

*'Yes, I do – we don't run away just because some bully is at the school gate threatening to take our sweets. We stand our ground.'*

*Bedrich blinked. 'I wouldn't underestimate the Nazis, they are far more than some schoolyard bully.'*

*Eva nodded. 'But they're thugs and soon someone will put a stop to it – there's no reason for us to worry about it here. He's just using the Jews as some kind of scapegoat for everything that went wrong for them after the war: people will see through it, uncle. And besides, this is Prague, it is such a multicultural city – I mean, most of my friends aren't Jewish, and they're absolutely* horrified – just as much as us – at the news. Michal says that everyone at the symphony feels the same way too.'

Anka nodded. 'Besides, apart from my visits to the synagogue on holy days, which I am made to do by myself because no one here is religious,' she said with a look of reprimand at her family, 'and Kaja's excellent challah bread, we're not that observant... even you sometimes eat pork,' she teased. 'Should we really worry so much?'

Bedrich shook his head, exasperated with them all. 'You think they care about that? How religiously we behave or not? I see it every day, there's a feeling, something stirring with his words, things are getting worse, even here.'

Eva's father shook his head. 'Bedrich, I know you are worried, but I don't think it will come to that. Not here. I don't think we should just run away just yet. It can't go on for much longer, this is a very different situation to Austria – they were very much affected after the war, their heads were turned by that madman wanting someone to blame. Here, I just don't see it happening, but if it looks like we will definitely be occupied, then you have my word, we will leave if we need to, all right?'

Bedrich stared at his brother, his dark eyes resigned. 'All right. But I worry that by then it will be too late.'

Otto clamped a hand on his brother's shoulder. 'You worry too much, Bedrich. Anyway if worst comes to worst I have faith in you and your connections to get us out of here.'

Bedrich laughed, but it didn't meet his eyes. 'Let's hope so, brother.'

# TWENTY-ONE

Eva stared at Herman, her heart thundering in her ears as she waited for him to reply.

When he spoke, she didn't hear it above the roar inside her ears.

'What?'

He touched her arm. 'He's alive, Eva.'

Eva started to breathe, but it was too fast and she couldn't control it – or the smile that ripped through her. The rush of adrenalin that made her want to run to find him. She was overcome. 'Alive!' Tears fell from her eyes in streams, making it hard to see.

'Where is he? Can I see him, can someone take me to him?'

Herman's eyes were grave. 'There's something you have to know.'

Her eyes snapped towards his, and a chill entered her heart. 'What?'

'There's a man that *might* be Michal who is alive, one of the *Kapos* – one we can trust – said it was possible it's him – they aren't sure, though. They're keeping him in a room by the hospital. That's all I could find out.'

Eva's eyes were huge. 'I have to go to him, somehow.'

Herman looked at her, then his eyes scanned the distance, checking to see if they were being watched, and he nodded. 'I can't get you in, I'm sorry – even Vincent – my *Kapo*, can't – but your friend might, the one who works at the hospital.'

Eva looked at him. 'Why do you say that?'

'Because Vincent said he saw her with the guard – the one who put the man in that cell.'

'Hinterschloss?'

'The other one, Meier.'

Eva waited for Sofie to get home – she was on the nightshift, and the wait felt interminable. Finally, at three in the morning, she arrived, and Eva told her what she'd found out.

'And Meier is keeping him there?' Sofie sounded shocked.

Eva shrugged. 'That's what Herman said. Look, can you find out?'

Sofie nodded. 'Yes, and I'll make sure you can see him – if it's him.'

Eva looked at her friend. 'Sofie, I can't ask you to put yourself in that kind of risk – people are already starting to talk about Meier. It's dangerous.'

Sofie shook her head. 'I can handle it. Trust me. There's nothing to worry about.'

'So, he hasn't forced you or anything?'

Sofie shook her head. The truth was he had begun to push harder, he was always at the hospital, and he wasn't satisfied with simple kisses any more. He found excuses to take her away, to lead her to a nearby storeroom, and push his hands up her skirt, his hard fingers touching her roughly, in what he no doubt presumed was pleasure, taking her hand and putting them in his trousers, while he kissed her. She knew that if she managed to convince Meier to help, she would have to sleep with him 'He's a gentleman,' she lied. 'I'll get you to see this man – Michal or whoever he is, all right? But he might not be – and trust me you don't want to get your hopes up.'

Eva closed her eyes. It was too late for that.

*

It took a few days, but Sofie told her to go to the hospital after curfew. 'You'll have to dodge the spotlights, but you can make it. I'll be there waiting for you – give Maria this,' she said, handing her a large wedge of salami, which Eva squirrelled up her sleeve quickly.

She nodded. Maria was bribable, they'd proven it a few times in exchange for washroom privileges and other necessities.

'Thank you.'

She shook her head. 'Don't thank me yet. But maybe you can see him, even if it's – for the last time. The man – Michal – if it is him – was beaten. Badly. He's been taken to a holding area near the hospital. Apparently, he intervened when some boy was caught stealing extra food, they punished him instead.'

Tears slipped from Eva's eyes at this. That sounded like something he would do. Sofie touched her arm. 'Meier says he looks in bad shape – one of the other guards beat him – the only reason he's alive is because one of his friends begged Meier, and he took him there. He doesn't know his name, and that boy has been moved so he couldn't ask. He hadn't been able to get much out of him to find out who he is.'

Eva closed her eyes in horror, and in hope.

Eva slipped out in the dead of night. It was freezing cold, and oddly still, despite the floodlights. In the distance, she could make out the sounds of walking feet. The *Kapo*, Maria, was waiting for her and she'd accepted the salami, with the briefest nod. 'I don't want to know why you need to go – it's better if I don't.'

The footsteps died down, and Maria held a finger to her lips. 'Go,' she said, 'If anyone asks, I'll tell them I sent you.'

Eva nodded.

At every point as she walked she feared that someone would find her out of her barracks and would kill her. She didn't know what she feared more. Being killed or being killed before she saw Michal again. Or getting there and finding it wasn't him.

*I just need to make it there to see him*, she thought as she ran. Her heartbeat pounded in her ears. Despite the cold night, and the wind howling through the camp, sweat broke out on her forehead. She could smell her own fear. It was rank, and feral. She swallowed as she neared the spotlights, waiting for someone to shout out, tell her to stop – all the while, looking over her shoulder. A sound in the background made her whirl around, whatever it was made a skittering sound on the ground. A rat. She thought she might vomit in her relief. She kept pushing, kept running, fighting for air in her lungs, her legs burning. A stitch twisted her side, and she pressed her fingers against it and kept going. As she neared the hospital, she heard voices, and the sound of muffled footsteps behind her, she twisted around and had to clutch her chest as her breathing became more ragged. It was Meier. Her knees buckled, and she had to put her head between them, being sick on the ground.

When she'd straightened there was a look of revulsion on his face. 'Sorry,' she said.

He didn't acknowledge this, but his expression softened somewhat. 'You're late. Come, don't make me regret this.'

She shook her head. 'You won't.'

He nodded, and she followed behind the guard, wondering if she could trust him, as he slipped towards a darkened passage, just behind the hospital, away from the lights. Eva's heart thundered in her ears.

'You have half an hour,' he said, before unlocking a storeroom as he pushed her inside. Eva's heartbeat was loud in her ears.

'No crying, keep it quiet – or I won't be able to get you out again, understand?'

Eva nodded, and the door shut behind her with a thud, making her jump. She blinked in the darkness, her eyes blinded from the light outside. As her eyes adjusted, she saw shapes in the shadows. The smell was sour, like sickness and stale urine.

Eva stepped forward, seeing alongside the wooden wall a human shape lying on the ground. She rushed over, falling onto her knees with a thud. Was it him? Was it Michal?

Her hands gently turned his shoulder. Her throat constricted as she turned his face towards her, then blinked. It was utterly mutilated. Tears fell unbidden from her eyes. She couldn't tell if it was him, not at all. He had been beaten to within an inch of his life. His face was bloody, eyes swollen, lips huge and busted. There were black shadows beneath his eyes, and a criss-cross of gashes. She noted too that he held out his arms and leg to an angle, both were badly broken, the skin on his hand and foot swollen and discoloured.

She touched his uninjured arm, and his eyes opened faintly, then closed again.

'Michal?' she asked, her fingers shaking as she touched his shorn hair. It didn't look brown, but it was hard to tell, as it was covered in dirt and blood. There was barely a part of this poor soul that didn't seem broken.

There was a groaning sound, and Eva blinked, touching his arm again.

'Are you… Michal. Michal Adami?'

There was another loud groaning sound again.

But there was something there she recognised, wasn't there? She looked at the hands. The shape of his head. *Maybe.* She swallowed, looked down at his hand. Was that familiar? She didn't know. Tears slipped from her eyes, and she wiped them away angrily. She couldn't help the sob that wracked through her body.

'Are you Michal?' she whispered again, desperately.

He made a strange sound.

'What did you say?'

It sounded almost like 'leave'.

She touched his arm, 'You want me to go?' The hand lifted for a moment then went still.

She thought her heart might break in two.

There was a loud bang from the door, and Meier's voice hissed. 'One minute!'

She looked down at the man on the ground, and his eyes closed. He'd passed out. She shook his undamaged arm.

The door started to open, and Eva's lips crumpled. She shook the man before her, 'Please, please, just tell me who you are, then I'll leave you alone,' she said, tears running fast down her cheeks, as she gasped for air.

There was a groaning sound again, and Meier's boots were entering the room. Eva closed her eyes. It wasn't him, she'd seen something that wasn't there. He wanted her to leave.

She stood up to go, her legs unsteady, feeling suddenly weak, and spent, tears falling in great choking sobs that she wasn't able to fight. As she made to go, the man's hand shot out to stop her, and suddenly the groaning sound rose in volume, and became a word. *'Eee… Eva?'*

# TWENTY-TWO

## Prague, Winter 1938

*Eva and Michal got married on a cold November morning at the registry office. Eva wore her mother's pearls, her grandmother's cream gown which they altered, and her cousin Mila was her bridesmaid. Despite the fear of German occupation and her uncle Bedrich's worried eyes about their future, it was one of the happiest days of her life.*

*Eva moved into Michal's tiny studio in the heart of Prague, and they settled into their new lives. They bought new furniture and she painted pictures for the walls.*

*Eva went to art school, Michal to the orchestra, and in the evenings, they went to her parents, to friends. They attended the cinema, concerts, and were as happy as two young people in love could be.*

*But everything was about to change, and quickly. The news was announced at six thirty in the morning. The Germans were coming. They were told to keep calm. They watched from their balcony in horror as the Germans rolled into their beloved city with their tanks and their hob-nailed boots. It was snowing, winter in Prague, and the winter would last well after the sun finally came again.*

*Every day afterwards there were new orders from the German Reich. Soon they were to discover that everything that was ill in this world was a result, the Germans maintained, of the Jews.*

*'Have you seen this rubbish?' muttered Michal in disgust as he looked at the newspaper, which was suddenly full of anti-Semitic nonsense. 'It's like they were just waiting for the chance to spew this bile.'*

*The orders for Jews continued. Soon they were nothing more than second-class citizens. Almost overnight the population – now called the protectorate of Bohemia and Moravia – were being told that their friends and neighbours, the Jews, were not to be trusted. In the beginning, Eva and her family weren't even sure what they were allowed to do – so frequently did the orders appear.*

*Jews couldn't go to the cinema, theatres, parks, concerts, they were forbidden from attending schools. Eva found herself suddenly unable to continue her studies.*

*She looked at Michal, tears in her eyes. 'I had the best grade of the year, that's what they said, before they told me I had to leave.'*

*He held her in his arms. 'This can't last, my love. They won't be able to get away with this for long. Soon they will get kicked out. The allies will intervene, it won't go on forever.'*

*He was right, by September war had been declared.*

In Eva's family, there was talk of going somewhere else, to take up Bedrich's offer – and go to England. But still they thought that things would get better.

But things only got worse. Soon there were signs. *Juden nicht zuganglich* – no Jews allowed. In all restaurants, cafés and bars. Businesses couldn't be owned by Jews.

Eva's mother said, 'They were defeated in the first war – they will be again. We just need to bide our time.'

Michal was let go from the symphony, and their landlord decided it was safer renting to non-Jews. They had no choice but to move in with Eva's family, into her old room.

Soon Michal wasn't the only man in the family without a job. They made the best of it. Eva's father learnt how to cook and Michal became the best cleaner, they boasted that they would become home-makers.

They got by with help from some of their non-Jewish friends, who sent money and parcels of food.

The final indignity was wearing the large yellow 'J' on the front of their coats, for Jude. They had to get in the back of any train, third class. Unlike their friends. Then in October the rumours began. The whispers about transports, and the decision to send the Jews away.

They tried their best not to worry, but when the letter came for Michal in the November, on the day of their first wedding anniversary, telling him to present himself to the Veletrh, the Trade Fair, where he would be processed for transportation, she broke down. 'I'll go too. You can't go without me.'

# TWENTY-THREE

Eva started to cry. 'Michal.'

He nodded and the action caused him to groan again.

'It's you,' she breathed in fear and wonder.

His hand came out to touch her – her face, her hair, his fingers shaking. Seeing her, registering that it was her, had revived him.

His voice came out slow. Eva suspected that his ribs must have been cracked from where he'd been beaten. 'I – I didn't know if I would.'

'Shhh,' she said. Speaking was tiring him out.

A tear rolled down her cheeks. 'I told you I would find you again.'

His swollen lips twitched. 'You did.'

Meier was growing impatient. 'Come on, time to go.'

She closed her eyes, how could she leave him now? 'Just a moment longer,' she begged. The guard grunted. 'Thirty seconds, say goodbye.'

Eva's heart thudded, and she lent down to kiss Michal. Despite how weak he was, his grip was firm. 'N-no, don't,' he protested.

'Come on,' said Meier, pulling her away, roughly. 'This has gone on long enough.'

She staggered to her feet, sure her heart was breaking at being torn from him. After all this time. 'I will come back,' she promised Michal.

*

Sofie was waiting for her just behind the hospital block. Meier looked at her, and his eyes pinned her to the spot, they shared a look. She was going to pay for this, she knew. 'Can you give us a moment,' she begged. Touching his arm.

A muscle flexed in his jaw, but he nodded. 'This has already taken too long,' he admonished, but he waited in the shadows nonetheless. There was a flare of a match, and they could smell the scent of a cigarette being lit.

Sofie eyed the young guard, then turned back to her friend. 'It was him?'

'Yes,' said Eva, and she couldn't help the smile that flitted across her face, replaced quickly by worry. He was alive, but who knew for how long.

Sofie breathed out. 'Thank God for that.'

Eva nodded. 'He's in bad shape though,' and her lips began to tremble.

'I'll ask Geneva – the *Blockalteste* – to check him out.'

Eva's eyes widened. 'Sofie, can we trust her?'

It was a moment before she answered. 'Yes, I think so.'

In the past few weeks, Sofie had become her apprentice, and many of the tasks the gynaecologist had asked her to perform in secret, involved trying to treat and help some of the women that had been tortured by Mengele. If he found out, they'd both be shot. The upside of having Geneva know her secret – that she wasn't a real nurse – was that she knew hers. What was one more risk?

There was a grunt from behind, and the sound of a boot stamping on the ground.

'Play time is over, girls,' said Meier, coming forward.

He looked at Eva. 'Wait there for me,' he said, indicating a few short paces. 'Turn your back.'

Eva did, from behind she could hear the sound of shuffling, the sound of her friend being pushed toward a wall, and then muffled grunts. Eva closed her eyes in horror as she realised what was happening. She couldn't believe that he was doing it there in the open. Till she realised, perhaps he wanted her to know. Her friend had called him a gentleman. Clearly, he was done with that, or it's what she wanted Eva to think, not to worry for her. She felt fresh tears prick her eyes, and she had to ball her fists. What had she got her friend into?

That night when Sofie slipped into the bunk beside her, Eva turned wide awake eyes on her friend.

'Sofie – I—' She didn't know what to say.

'Don't, *Kritzelei*. You found Michal, which makes it all worth it. I'm glad he's alive.'

'But Meier—'

'Is a little boy, playing power games.'

'I thought,' Eva frowned, 'I thought maybe he was different. He said he loves you.'

Sofie snorted. 'It's not love if you feel the need to control it. Anyway, he was just trying to prove a point.'

'To who – you or me?'

'Both, probably.'

'Which is?'

'That he can do what he likes. That he'll help so long as I pretend that he's the love of my life. That I'm overcome with lust for him every time I see him.'

Eva swallowed. She hated this. 'I'll find another way, Sofie – this is just too much, it's not fair.'

'No, *Kritzelei* – it's too late anyway – at least this way we get something out of it. He might be an arrogant fool, but he's not rough with me if I do what he asks, and he sticks to his word. Besides, he can help us.'

'But what do you get, Sofie?'

'I get to know that I did everything I could to help my friend. The way she once stood in front of a man who was going to sentence me to death and risked herself in the process. It's what we do, isn't it?'

Eva sighed. 'I'd rather get attacked by ten more gendarmes than have you go through this.'

Sofie gave her a half smile. Sofie would no doubt have been dead if Eva hadn't intervened back in Terezín. It's not something she would ever forget.

'What's happened with Meier was going to happen, eventually. At least we've got something out of him as a result.'

Eva snuggled against her shoulder, and Sofie continued. 'Besides, if I hadn't – I wouldn't have been able to get Geneva in to see him.'

Eva looked up, her eyes fearful.

'How is he?'

'He has a few broken bones, and cracked ribs, but no internal injuries.'

Eva blinked.

'It's a good thing, *Kritzelei*.'

'Thank you,' she said.

The words didn't seem big enough for all that her friend had done, all that she had risked.

Sofie squeezed her hand back.


It took another three days before Eva got word through Sofie that Michal was doing better. The waiting was a strange kind of limbo – on one hand she knew now where he was, and that there was a chance that he would live. On the other, he was badly injured and needed her, and it ate her alive.

'He's more conscious now – seeing you really did something to him. He's more lucid. I think he's going to pull through,' said Sofie, her eyes hopeful.

Eva breathed out.

'Meier said he will try get you in tomorrow night.'

The next evening, Meier led her through to the cell. It was dark, but the room had changed slightly. The smell was less sour and the stench of urine had gone.

Michal was sitting up in the corner. The bruises on his face had started to turn purple and green. His one eye was still pretty much shut. He smiled when he saw her, and there was just the smallest hint of a dimple. Seeing it made her throat catch.

'Oh, my love,' she said, throwing herself into his arms.

He gasped in pain.

She pulled a face. 'I'm sorry!'

He shook his head, refusing to let her go. 'Don't be,' he said, then cupped her face in his hands, drinking her in.

Eva felt nervous as his gaze raked over her short hair, her skinny face and limbs. She worried about the gap where her tooth was missing on the side of her mouth. She knew she looked a fright. She raised a shaking hand to her hair. 'I look a bit different too,' she said, giving him a half smile.

He shook his head, then pressed his battered lips against her forehead. 'You are the most beautiful thing I have seen in two years, trust me.'

Tears coursed dirty tracks down her face, and she kissed his uninjured hand, clutching it to her as she knelt before him. He touched her short hair, ran his fingers along her skull, making goosebumps rise on her skin in pleasure.

'How did you find me?' he asked. 'It's like a miracle.'

Eva nodded. It was. The miracle's name was Herman. She told him about the photograph, of meeting him.

'But why are you here, did they send you on a transport?'

She looked down, then whispered, 'I volunteered to come.'

When she looked up, there were tears coursing down his face, as if that thought caused him more pain than his injuries.

'I wasn't the only wife to do it,' she said, defensively.

'Oh, Eva, what was getting me through this hell was knowing that at least you weren't here, you were back in Terezín… you were safe.'

She touched his face, then she kissed his split lips gently. 'Nowhere in this war is safe, my love, even Terezín. It was worth it to find you, for us to be together again. People die every day just from thirst or disease. What we need is to be with each other, to know we're alive – that's how we'll survive.'

*

184

Due to Sofie's relationship with Meier, Eva managed to see Michal every few nights, and to get him more food. Sofie organised cheese and salami and potatoes – it was like a small feast, which they shared together.

Every day, he seemed to get that little bit better. That little bit stronger. They didn't get much time together, just a half hour here and there every few evenings. But it was enough. A magic time that was just for them. She lived for those half hours. Getting through her long twelve-hour shifts with thoughts of his eyes, his lips. A few moments of pleasure in the bleakest of surroundings that got her through the very long days.

The first time they made love, on the dirty floor, Eva had to be as gentle as it was possible to be, not to hurt his ribs or his arms and knee.

She realised that it was possible to be happy, in even the darkest of times.

\*

After they'd been reunited for two weeks, Eva's work unit was moved outside to work on building roads. It was a three-kilometre trek there and back. It was tough, back-breaking work, but with the sun filtering through the clouds, and falling on her shoulders, Eva was able for a moment to lose herself in the memory of her husband's arms. It was a dangerous game, she knew. If any of the other guards caught them, they'd be killed.

But for now, it was bliss.

As they worked, she hummed. Someone started to sing a song, and the others joined in, before one of the *Kapos* told them to keep it down.

The transports ran day and night, taking people to and from Auschwitz, she barely even noticed them anymore, too tired and too hungry to worry. Until she returned that evening after the *Appell*, and found Sofie waiting for her in the barracks, a worried look on her pretty face.

'Have they changed your shift?' asked Eva, surprised to find her here.

Her friend shook her head. 'No, I'm still on a night shift – I came here quickly, used an excuse – said I had to fetch Geneva's medical bag, but I needed to tell you.'

Eva felt dread fill her insides. 'Tell me what?'

Her straight-talking friend fumbled. 'Oh, *Kritzelei*—'

'What?' said Eva, her heart starting to pound.

'Michal has been sent away. Meier arranged it.'

Eva closed her eyes, feeling faint. 'Sent where?'

'Some factory – in Freiberg.'

'He said it was for the best,' said Sofie, not looking her friend in the eye. Not telling her about how she'd shouted at Meier when he'd told her what he'd done, and how he'd knocked her off her feet with a backhand, hissing in her ear, 'I like being with you, but don't forget who is in charge.' He'd shaken his head and sneered. 'Maybe Hinterschloss was right, he said I was being led by what's between your thighs. But I'm the man in this relationship, do you understand?'

She'd nodded, and apologised, hating herself for it. Hating him too. 'Good,' he'd said, and hadn't bent down to help her up. She realised then just how much the other guard had been feeding poison into his ear. Perhaps it was this place too – was it any surprise that whatever humanity he might have had coming in was wearing thin now?

She looked up at Eva, and touched her arm. 'He'll have a chance. They say it's better in the factories, much better than here.'

Eva nodded. It was true. Keeping him here was a danger, especially in his condition. She was grateful for that.

'Thank you, Sofie – I can't imagine it's been easy, I feel terrible at all you've risked—'

'Don't, *Kritzelei*, it's fine,' protested Sofie. She didn't want her friend to worry about her.

It wasn't fine but Eva dropped it, Sofie clearly didn't want to talk about it. She didn't know how she would ever be able to pay her back.

'Can I say goodbye?'

Sofie gazed at her, her face stricken. 'He's already gone, I'm sorry.'

It was safer that way, Eva knew. The further her husband was moved from Hinterschloss, and here, the better his chances

187

of survival. Still, it seemed unbelievably cruel that they had found each other after all this time, only to be ripped apart. Still, they were alive, for now, that's all that mattered.

*

In the morning, though, she knew that she had a new worry, something to distract her from the pain of losing her husband once again. Hinterschloss stared down at her, with his yellow eyes, a cruel smile about his lips. 'Our translator,' he said.

Eva stared.

'Answer me when I speak to you!'

'You didn't ask me a question.'

His eyes widened, and he stepped forward. Before she knew anything else, he'd slammed the butt of his rifle against her head, and she went falling backwards into the dirty, churned-up mud. Her ears ringing, her head screamed through the pain. While she was down he knelt beside her and hissed, 'So you think you can sneak around here at night without me finding out. Your little friend might have got Meier to convince me not to *kill you* – but I didn't promise that I'd make your life worth living.' Then he kicked her hard in the ankle, till she felt something crack. In her pain, anger, and fear, he stood up and addressed her *Kapo,* Maria. 'This one is on half-rations from now on.'

*

Vanda and the other girls helped Eva up. Maria looked at her and shook her head. 'Silly girl,' she snapped. 'Was it worth all this?'

Eva shrugged. 'Yes, probably.'

Maria snorted and walked on, leaving her standing in her blood, her ankle throbbing in pain. Eva stared after her retreating back. Maria had helped her before through a series of bribes, but with Hinterschloss out for blood, she wouldn't risk her own neck. Eva had lost an important ally, and it was going to make things even harder.

Using a dirty scarf as a bandage for her ankle, Eva managed to half hobble away to join the work unit for the three-kilometre walk. It was agony, and it would be even worse with almost no food in her belly. She thought of Michal, of her family, picturing her mother's soft smile, her father's kind eyes, Bedrich's craggy face, and she took a deep breath, as someone prodded her to keep moving; somehow, she did.

# TWENTY-FOUR

*Prague, 1940*

'You can't go without me,' Eva repeated, staring at Michal, her eyes fierce.

He shook his head, green eyes full of fear and remorse.

'You can't come with me, Eva. They're only taking the men—'

'No! They can't separate us like this, it's too cruel,' she gasped.

He held her close. 'Listen to me, they need men to build the stupid concentration camp first, turn it from a garrison town into a holding pen for us, that's what your uncle Bedrich said.'

Her uncle found out these things, no one knew how.

'Can't we just get out – out of Prague – escape to the mountains, the countryside, somewhere?'

'I don't think so, no one will take us – and they have our names. We would need different papers, different identities, it's too late.'

Eva's eyes widened. 'Amira got them. We can ask her mother.'

Amira was a friend from school, who had left the city shortly after the first orders began, when people still believed that they were panicking for nothing.

190

Her father shook his head.

'She knew that priest – but they've taken him away for questioning. They want us gone. Mr Rubenstein is leaving tomorrow too.'

Eva gasped. He was their oldest neighbour. The one who had shown her on the steps outside their flat how to tie her shoelaces when she was five. It was like the world had gone mad.

'Eva listen to me, the thing is—' said her father, 'while I wish they were only sending the men, and you women could be spared this, I think they will be sending every Jew eventually, and for now we know where most people in Prague are going, which is a good thing. So, when the time comes, it will most likely be in Terezín. I'm sure then we will all be together again.'

'How can you be sure?'

'I can't be. But we just have to keep the faith.'

Eva nodded. It would be hard though.

\*

In the morning, they took Michal to the Trade Fair Palace, where he was to be processed before departure. They could only go so far as the gates, Eva was pushed back, crying.

Two weeks later, the letter came for the rest of them.

Eva was both horrified and relieved, at least she would see Michal again. She began packing her allowed fifty kilograms of luggage with determination.

# TWENTY-FIVE

The hot sun beat down on their backs as they worked. Eva's eye was purple and still swollen, a new present from Hinterschloss the week before. Her ankle was broken, and it hurt whenever she stood on it.

By late summer, Eva went from working on roads to working in fields. With her rations cut shorter she only got her portion of thin, watery soup, with nothing much else in it.

Starvation would have been certain if not for the kindness of the women in her barrack, and past favours that could now be repaid. Noemi, a friend she'd made when she'd first arrived in Auschwitz, had been moved to kitchen duties, and she gave her extra bread and potato peelings and whatever else she could, including a wedge of cheese.

'I won't forget that I got this mug because of you,' she whispered, pressing them into her red, chapped hands at night when she passed her. Eva was so grateful she could cry.

Sofie had helped to bandage Eva's foot properly, and had managed to sneak her some painkillers, which were like gold dust here. But as the long, hot summer days marched on, thirst, a constant companion, was another major problem in the camp. When the heavens opened above their heads, many of the inmates would rejoice, cupping the precious liquid in their dirty hands and slurping it down.

In the distance, there was the rumble of aeroplanes. Air raids had begun. The whispers that the war was turning against the Germans soon followed.

As Autumn arrived, it brought with it the first snap of cold weather, and frost, and Eva felt ill. What little food she had in her stomach wouldn't stay down. She crept out of her bunk in the dead of the night, and weakly leaning against the wall outside, vomited what was left of the black bread they'd given them in the evening.

There was a sound behind her, and Eva started. It was Maria, smoking a cigarette.

Eva closed her eyes. 'I think it's some kind of a bug,' she said. 'There's one going around.'

Maria nodded, then looked at her appraisingly. 'I wonder if it's not something else.'

Eva frowned, confused. 'What do you mean?'

'Morning sickness.'

Eva blinked. Pregnant? That couldn't be possible, could it?

Not on these rations. She hadn't had a period in months, they'd stopped shortly after she'd arrived in Auschwitz.

Maria shrugged. 'It happens – one of my girls here fell pregnant. Geneva – the *Blockalteste* – took care of it.'

Eva felt a chill run down her spine. 'Took care of it?' she repeated.

Maria didn't explain further, she didn't need to.

Eva closed her eyes in horror. 'I'm not pregnant,' she said.

'You better hope not,' she said, shaking her head and extinguishing her cigarette on the floor. 'Now, get back to bed.'

*

When she slipped back inside her bunk, she fit her body next to Sofie's. Her friend's hair had started to grow back. Dark blonde, with a slight curl. She hadn't noticed the curl before. She wondered absently as she lay in bed, fighting the nausea, if it was a result of being here that had changed it. Sofie shifted, opening her dark eyes to look at her. 'You still feeling sick?' she whispered.

Eva nodded.

Sofie patted her arm, then closed her eyes. 'Try get some sleep.'

'Maria asked if I was pregnant.'

Sofie's eyes opened again. She blinked.

'I can't be, can I?'

Sofie's eyes were wide, and full of fear. She swallowed. 'Whatever they put in the food, and the rations generally stops it – but there have been some cases – not everyone's body reacts the same way.'

Her eyes were full of the horror that she had witnessed at the hospital. She didn't tell her friend about the sorts of things she saw. The things that the doctor, Mengele, did. His experiments – some of which he did on pregnant women. There had been one woman – Geneva said he'd injected something into her cervix. They didn't know what had happened to her afterwards, she'd got lost in the system somehow. Most of the others had their foetuses removed or were gassed.

'Oh, *Kritzelei*,' she whispered, clutching her hand.

Eva closed her eyes in sudden fear. She'd been hoping that Maria was just scaremongering. Hoped that it wasn't possible.

Then something occurred to her. 'But it was evening when I started feeling sick – so it can't be.'

Sofie laughed softly, but there was no humour in it. 'I'm afraid that the term "morning sickness" is a misnomer, some people feel sick their whole first trimester or longer.'

Sofie remembered feeling ill for weeks on end, tired too. She'd been scared of what the future had in store – scared to be a single mother despite her tough-talk to her family, but whenever she'd felt Tomas move inside her, it had seemed like he was giving her courage. She wiped away a surreptitious tear now.

'Oh,' said Eva, feeling her heart start to pound. 'I didn't know that.'

Sofie squeezed her hand. For her friend's sake, she hoped that it wasn't true. 'If you are pregnant, this is going to be impossible.'

Eva shook her head, felt her stomach. 'No, if I'm pregnant then it makes all the difference.'

Sofie looked shocked.

'Because then out of all this something good happened, and I will fight like hell to make sure my child lives.'

Her friend clutched her hand, she didn't tell her she was daydreaming, as usual, she didn't have to.

# TWENTY-SIX

*Prague, 1940*

*It took them three days to get to Terezín. Eva had travelled with her family, each with fifty kilograms of luggage. They had waited around in the Trade Fair Palace, where they stayed for two days on dirty mattresses with all their luggage, before the trams arrived. The days were long and interminable, while they waited with their transport numbers, and then they were stripped of most of their valuables. On the third morning before they boarded the train, they listened in shock as a German officer gave them a speech to say that they were now travelling to a promised land, a ghetto where the people there would build for themselves a place free from persecution. They were told that they should be happy and thankful that they were some of the first to be going – they were real pioneers.*

*Eva and her parents shared bemused looks as they at last boarded the trains, their luggage at their feet.*

*After several stop starts, they travelled to a large camp. When they arrived, there were more shocks in store, as Eva's father was torn from their grasp, and ushered away.*

'No!' shouted Anka, as Otto was forced to follow the other men.

'I'll be all right, my loves,' said Otto. 'It's just for now.'

Eva bit back a sob as she watched him being led away with the men, then her arm was tugged, and she and the other women were being herded towards the women's sections.

She held on to her mother, who looked like a balloon with a puncture. 'We'll be strong for Papa, and Michal. We'll see them soon,' she promised her.

Her mother stared, wiping her eyes. 'Where have they taken us?'

\*

Eva and her mother followed the other women to the women's quarters, and a gendarme told them to pick beds. Eva sat down with her mother. They didn't even have their luggage. Around them other women had set up little stations. There were even pots and pans, and washing hanging on the windows.

Eva was exhausted. It had been a long few days. Together, they climbed onto the bed, arms around each other, and despite their new surroundings, their worries of when they would see their men again, and the whispers of the other women, they were soon asleep.

\*

She woke up, to her mother roughly shaking her arm. 'Come quick.'

'What?'

Her mother put a hand over her mouth. 'Shh, just come.'

She followed after to the courtyard where a group of men were going past with trolleys full of luggage, then found herself being whipped around, then lifted off her feet, and hugged fiercely.

Michal.

She sank into his strong arms, fighting back a sob. Drinking in his face, his eyes, his hair, which had somehow grown longer and curlier, over his collar. He looked the same, maybe a little thinner. 'You're okay?'

He smiled, showing a dimple. 'I am now,' he said, holding her tight.

She touched his face. 'But they are treating you okay?'

'Yes, it's not too bad. I'm employed as a builder, but they have asked me to play them the violin too – they say it calms the other men.'

She grinned, she liked thinking of him getting to play still. 'Does it?'

He shrugged. 'A little.' He leant in for a lingering kiss. A guard came past and he let her ago, the gendarme, however, seemed to be very interested in something on the floor. She frowned before she understood, he was pretending to look the other way, and she found herself oddly touched.

'Can you come again?

'Yes, tomorrow.'

She smiled.

# TWENTY-SEVEN

As the weeks passed, Eva knew she was pregnant, it was inescapable. Her life became about trying her best to conceal it, and to protect her unborn child.

At night she sat, eyes wide, feeling her belly under cover of darkness. It was tiny, barely more than a small bulge. If she stood naked it would be hard to tell for sure, but Geneva had confirmed it, after a short examination in the *Blockalteste*'s rooms on Sofie's behest.

'I think you should let me abort it,' said the tall woman, peering at her, not unkindly.

Eva swallowed, shook her head. Tears fell from her eyes. 'Are you going to tell them?'

Geneva shook her head. 'No. I should – that's what they expect us to do – but I won't. They've stopped killing pregnant mothers now.'

Eva blanched. She'd known that they had done that but to hear it so bluntly took her breath away.

'Look, I'll leave it with you – think about it – I'd say you're due in about February next year, that's five months away, you're not going to have that much time.'

200

Eva blinked, nodding. She was four months pregnant. She left promising that she would let her know. But she had already decided. She'd decided on the day she'd suspected that she was pregnant.

That night while she lay in her bunk, she whispered to her unborn child. 'I don't know how you came about in all of this, my darling, but you are a miracle, of that I have no doubt,' she whispered, while everyone slept.

It was a strange thing, Eva realised, being pregnant. It was like having some new hope coursing through her veins. While she'd been so focused on finding her husband, and imagining that one day they might make it out of this – that seed had found its way inside of her and created new life already. She touched her belly and thought, *If it's a girl I'm going to name you, Naděje.* It meant hope.

There were other worries too, like Sofie who came down with tonsillitis, which was brought on, no doubt, by the lack of proper nutrition.

Meier had been moved on to some other detail, after he'd been caught by a senior officer giving extra food to Sofie.

In many ways, she was relieved, Meier had grown pushier, more demanding, his actions emulating Hinterschloss's. He seemed to swing from day to day, being kind one moment, cruel the next. It was as if he couldn't decide if she were his girlfriend, or his whore. She felt a bit like both. Whatever the case, once she'd slept with him, there had been no turning back, and no escaping him. While he had been good to her in the sense that he always brought her extra food, it came at a high price, and that had grown to include slaps and bruises over the weeks, as well as Hinterschloss's renewed interest in her, as the guard found every excuse to test his friend's merchandise when he passed her way.

'Meier has grown up a lot, little Bette Davis,' he said, his hand sliding towards her groin. 'It makes me wonder about this man-maker,' he said, then laughed at her horrified eyes.

With Meier out of the way, she hoped that Hinterschloss would lose interest too. She had begun already to fear what she might end up doing to Meier, she had dreams of killing him as he lay spent in her arms.

Eva was terrified that her friend would get pneumonia, which was rampaging through the camp along with Scarlet fever and other illnesses, due to the lack of hygiene and poor diet. She fed her her portion of bread each night and while Sofie spent two days in bed, Eva cared for her as best as she could.

'No, don't give me your food, *Kritzelei*, you're working – and *expecting* – you need it.'

'What I need is for my bossy friend to live, and get better, okay?' said Eva, giving her some water from her mug. She'd got some painkillers from Geneva for her as well.

Sofie closed her eyes. Her throat was on fire as she whispered, 'If I don't make it through this, you'll go and get Tomas, you'll raise him, won't you?'

Eva turned to look at Sofie, her eyes concerned. 'Don't speak like that, we'll get out of this alive, together. Like we said, okay?'

Sofie shut her eyes. 'I'm serious, *Kritzelei*, please. If I don't make it – you'll need to go to Bergenz – it's on the Austrian border, it's where Lotte lived. I've had a lot of time to think about it – she wouldn't have had a chance to go far to find an orphanage if that's where she took him – so it has to be close by. Maybe a nunnery, one of the churches – who knows. Or a non-Jewish friend, she had a few of those, you'll have to ask around. The midwife who delivered Tomas was called Liesl, I can't remember her surname – but you could ask her. They should have records if she did it officially…'

'Sofie—'

'*No, Eva*. It's important, listen to me. I haven't given up, and I'm sticking to our plan – but in case,' she swallowed, 'in case I don't survive I need you to do this. He might even be with Lotte's husband, Udo, if he's still alive. After what she did to my father and I – to Tomas – well, I just don't want my son to be raised by someone like that. I know she was afraid – God, it's probably not good of me, but still, I can't forgive it. I'm sorry. And I can't let her husband raise my son or have him live forever in an orphanage, I can't let that happen. Okay?

Promise me you'll go get him if you survive and I don't. You'll raise him as your own. Please?'

Eva took her friend's hands in hers, her eyes were full of tears. 'I will, I promise. Now eat.'

And Sofie did.

# TWENTY-EIGHT

*Terezín, December 1940–1942*

*At first family visits happened only once a week but soon, as time moved on and Eva and her family had been in Terezín for several weeks, there was more freedom and they could see them more regularly, though the men and women were still separated at night.*

*Eva started working in the kitchen gardens, and her daily life settled down into a routine.*

*It was bearable, because she was with her family, and she got to see Michal.*

*The New Year brought with it new arrivals. Every day there were new transports and friends and family and people they used to know crowded into the old town.*

*There were fears that there would soon be too many. Transports would begin sending them somewhere else. A whisper only of 'East'. It brought terror to all their hearts.*

*Eva and her mother were moved into a new barrack, but they were separated when her mother was put on a cleaning detail.*

She'd been at the camp for just under two months when she heard the news. Her mother came rushing at her, her eyes wide. 'It's Mila and Bedrich, they are here!'

They rushed towards the area of the Schleuse, but the wait for them was long, and the gendarmes sent her back to work. She couldn't wait to see her cousin.

When, at last, she saw her, she was shocked. Mila had grown thin, she looked ill. Her eyes were large and sad, but she embraced Eva firmly. 'I have missed you so much.'

Eva nodded. 'Me too. What happened?'

'Father tried to get us out – a last attempt, when they sent the papers to our flat. Arnold—' she closed her eyes, and tears leaked down her pretty face, 'and I followed him there in a car. We made it as far as the border. But they caught us, in the end. Arnold was killed.' Eva closed her eyes in horror. 'We were so close, Eva,' Mila said, her blue eyes pooling with tears.

'I'm sorry,' said Eva, gathering her cousin's thin frame in her arms. She led her to the barracks, and sat her down with her mother, who fussed over her, offering her something to eat. The light seemed to have gone out of Mila's eyes, as she climbed into bed. 'I just want to sleep,' she said. Eva nodded, and pulled a blanket over her cousin. Sharing a worried gaze with her mother. They had never seen her like this.

Uncle Bedrich was worried about his daughter. Otto, Eva's father, had got him a job as a handyman, but it was soon apparent that his skills could be used in other ways – carting off the dead *for instance. He didn't ask too many questions, and wasn't afraid to do the sort of work that needed someone with a strong stomach.*

*Eva managed to slip out and be with Michal as often as she could. It felt cruel to her that she had him, while her cousin pined away for Arnold. Summer arrived, and the camp was soon groaning with people – the facilities couldn't cope. The transports went every day. A shout ran out for her, and her father rushed towards her in the kitchen garden. 'Come quick, Eva.'*

*She rushed to follow, asking what was wrong, what was happening. 'Is it Mama? Michal? Mila? What's going on?'*

*'No time, even now, run.'*

*She raced after her father, her lungs burning, till they reached the trams. Her heart thudded in her chest. Michal was standing on the platform.*

*'No!' she shouted.*

*He turned, trying to come towards her, and the gendarme pushed him back, and herded him and the others onto the train. The doors slammed shut, and she sunk to her knees, watching in horror as it sped away from her.*

# TWENTY-NINE

Eva couldn't do hard labour anymore, not in her condition, and she managed to convince Maria to help get her assigned somewhere else, with a bribe of a large wedge of salami she managed to organise in exchange for her mug.

It was worth it.

She was put into the kitchen detail. In the long wintry months while she peeled potatoes and helped make the horrible soup, and cut up bread, it was possible to get extra portions of peelings, potato and small bits of other vegetables. It wasn't much but it was enough to keep her going. The work was tedious but it wasn't hard. Where she was was warm and dry, and she didn't need to stand all day which was the main thing.

Her tiny size, along with her loose clothing, hid her growing abdomen effectively, but she was terrified that she would have the baby here and that they would take it away from her before the war ended.

Every day, the rumours and whispers that the war was beginning to turn against the Germans, with the allied armies advancing ever closer to Auschwitz, spread like wildfire.

The commanders were beginning to see the end was near, and that things were not going to go the way they hoped. A month before, the crematoria were blown up. It was a massive explosion. They'd leapt from the bunks to see a fireball lighting up the night. There were cheers when people realised what had happened. 'Does this mean it's over?'

'There will no longer be gassings? We'll get to live!'

An old woman behind them snorted. 'Don't be such an idiot, if they're trying to cover their tracks before the Reds arrive, they won't leave us behind to tell the stories.'

Eva swallowed. The old woman had a point.

The air raids had gained in intensity. At night the shooting was relentless, turning the sky red.

'*Kritzelei*, I think it's going to be over in a matter of months, they say the allies are nearing the camp.' Then she looked down at Eva's belly and said. 'You just need to hang in there all right, they're coming soon.'

As winter marched on, order and discipline began to break down. There was an uprising and some of the crematoria workers – *Sonderkommandos*, men who had been forced to gas their fellow inmates – revolted. Perhaps they knew that they were going to be killed – it was they after all who had seen first hand what the SS had done. They led an uprising, killing several guards and managing to get away to nearby villages, but their escape was doomed, as they were all hunted down and killed.

The effect the turning war had on the guards was worrisome, though for the most part they were distracted and the hated *Appells* began to come to a halt, which was a relief. Even so, the guards were still a dangerous threat, and it was clear that they didn't want to leave any witnesses behind. Meier had left his other post and returned to Birkenau, which was both a blessing and a curse, as having him around offered a tiny shred of protection for Sofie and Eva. But it meant that Sofie was once again under his thumb.

The Soviet advance caused panic every day, and one day in January they bombed the food store. The SS began tearing down some of the fences, and getting rid of documentation, destroying evidence of what they'd done.

Hinterschloss took his vengeance out on those he could. They were marched out into the cold night air, and back again, and whenever one of the women tripped or fell he was there. Eva watched in horror as he took a pistol and shot Vanda in the head, her body slumped over – there was a dark pool of blood from her wound. It was agony losing their friend, and their bunk was a lonely place without her deep belly laugh and bright ginger hair.

As the weeks passed, work had stopped completely, which was a relief, but also a concern, because food was harder to get.

At eight months pregnant, Eva's stomach still barely showed. The baby was tiny, yet alive, somehow. Eva tried to give it encouragement, even as she scrounged on scraps, trying to convince herself that she wasn't starving.

Meier managed to get them some food, but he was distracted. He walked around as if he were in a daze most of the time, his blue eyes anxious, shadows beneath them.

'I don't think he quite realised that this place was evil – that what they were doing here was wrong – till he was told to start burning the evidence,' said Sofie.

Eva looked at her friend, trying to take that in – how someone could have seen all this every day and still not got that what they'd helped to do was beyond evil. 'So now he's sorry?' she asked.

'No, I just think maybe he's just starting to lose some of his blinkers, but perhaps not soon enough.'

She prayed that her baby would hold on. 'The Soviets are coming, just hang on a little while longer,' she told it.

\*

It was late at night when she was woken up by Sofie.

'Come on,' she whispered. 'There's someone here to see you.'

She got up, quickly, putting on her shoes in the freezing cold, her heart starting to race. Was it Michal? Was he back, somehow? Her heart flooded with hope. Only he would risk coming here. There were rumours that the work had stopped in the factories, perhaps they'd been sent back. Would he come straight here? she wondered, heart flooding with hope. It was foolish of him, but she would reprimand him later, after she hugged him till he begged her to stop.

She followed after Sofie. The *Kapo* was still asleep in her room, and Eva went outside, pausing in a mixture of confusion, disappointment and happiness as the light shone on an older figure with bushy eyebrows. It was Herman; behind him was Meier.

Herman greeted her with a quick hug.

'I didn't know if I'd ever see you again,' he said, his eyes sad.

'Me too.'

He reached out towards her. 'I asked Meier if I could come.' He darted a look at the guard, who looked away. 'I know I would have wanted someone to have done the same for me,' he said, his eyes full of remorse. 'It's bad news I bring, I'm sorry.'

Eva felt her heart start to pound. She didn't know if she wanted to hear it.

'Skelter returned from Freiberg last week – I'm afraid there was an accident. One of the wings collapsed in the aeroplane factory where he was working. They weigh a ton, there were a lot of injuries. I'm afraid Michal didn't make it.'

Eva felt her knees give out, a low keening wail wracked throughout her body, and she found it hard to breathe, she fell into the mud as her heart shattered within.

# THIRTY

Somehow Eva made it inside, she wasn't quite sure how, her legs were shaking uncontrollably, and tears coursed unchecked down her dirty cheeks. She stumbled towards her bunk, her knees wet and bruised from where she'd fallen in the snow. She didn't feel it. All around her the sounds of hundreds of women trying to sleep was like the muffled drone of bees, but all she could hear was the roaring in her own ears, that was calling Michal's name. Every time she closed her eyes she saw him. Saw that dimple that appeared whenever he touched her face.

How could he be gone? How could she go on without him?

Pain, like a knife to her abdomen, ripped through her and she gasped aloud, stumbling in her sodden clogs, doubling over, she clutched her stomach, then turned white in sudden, crippling fear.

She felt wet down her legs. The baby was coming. She closed her eyes in horror. 'Oh God, haven't you made me suffer enough?' she cursed. Fresh tears tracked her cheeks. 'I won't let you take my child too,' she vowed. '*I won't.*'

Sofie rushed to help her, 'Come on, just a few more steps, then you can lie down.'

Helga came down to help her.

Eva fought for breath, her head between her knees. At last she looked up, horror on her face as she whispered it aloud: 'I'm in labour.'

Sofie blinked. 'It must be shock.' She looked at the old woman and said, 'She just found out, Michal – he's gone.'

Helga's old face creased in sympathy, and she took Eva by the crook of her arm. 'Come on,' she said, helping her, her hands shaking in sudden fear. 'Let's get you to the top, you'll be less visible there, the girls won't mind.'

Two of the women from her bunk came to help her climb to the top. While Eva writhed, pain shooting through her, Helga explained what was happening. As Eva got into position, one of the women handed her a rolled-up piece of fabric. 'Put this in your mouth, bite down,' she suggested, not unkindly.

Eva nodded, tears leaking from her eyes. It would help keep her cries down in case Maria came to investigate, and called one of the guards.

'What are we going to do?' said Helga. 'I've never delivered a child before, have you?' she asked. They all shook their heads. Two had sat up to watch, to help, the others had their backs turned, refusing to get involved other than by keeping their mouths shut. In their eyes Sofie could see the fear they all shared. So much could go wrong in childbirth.

Sofie touched her shoulder, her hands shaking.

'I – I'm just going to get help.'

'No,' breathed Eva, opening her eyes in terror.

'*Kritzelei*, we have to. I've never done this, and I've seen…' She didn't finish, her eyes full of all the horrors she'd seen from malnourished women giving birth in the camp. 'Geneva will know what to do – how to give it the best chance, even though—'

Again, she didn't finish, her words breaking off. Eva was well aware that her baby was early.

Eva started to cry again, and Sofie touched her hair. 'It's going to be okay, *Kritzelei*,' she lied.

Eva's lips trembled. She didn't know how long she waited, the pain almost blinding as the contractions ripped through her, getting closer and closer together. Her tiny baby was determined to be born tonight.

Helga sat behind her, lending her what strength she had.

After what felt like an eternity she felt cool hands on her forehead, and looked up to see the *Blockalteste*'s calm black eyes. She began undressing her, and examining her body. 'It's going to come soon,' she said. They had brought with them all they could from Geneva's room, a pair of scissors sterilised in a kettle full of water and some fresh linens.

With Sofie acting as nurse – as the snow began to fall in thick drifts outside, the wind howling through the barren plains outside – they all knelt by her side as her baby entered the world in one of the most unwelcome places on earth.

Eva tried to sit up to see her child, and Helga held her back, her eyes worried as they all peered down at the tiny baby between her legs. They were all waiting for the cry.

Which did not come.

Eva closed her eyes, her breath coming in fast. 'Is – is the baby—?'

'I'm checking,' said Geneva, putting her ear to the baby's chest, tapping her slightly, but she didn't make a sound – they would soon find out that it *couldn't,* not really.

The baby fitted easily in Sofie's hands. It couldn't weigh more than two and half pounds.

'Breathing,' said Geneva at last. 'She's alive.'

Eva took in a deep breath. 'It's a girl,' she gasped, a smile butterflying across her face in relief, and unexpected joy.

Geneva nodded, cutting the cord, and wrapping the baby in a cloth and handing it to Eva very gently. The new mother sat up painfully to cradle her child.

'She is terribly small. Her lungs are very weak, I don't think she can cry,' said Geneva, her eyes dark and full of sympathy. 'I'm not sure if she will survive. But if she does, there might be other problems, her bones look very weak. I'm sorry.'

Eva's lip trembled as she held her baby gently in her arms, and stared down at the perfect, minuscule face, Michal's features stamped in miniature, and her heart felt like it might just burst.

'Naděje,' she breathed. 'You will live, I will make sure of it.'

Sofie touched her friend's arm, tears coursing down her cheeks. 'I will too.'

*

A few hours later, Eva's milk had arrived. It was a miracle. There were other women who'd had babies in Auschwitz, but without milk there was no way to feed them and death soon followed.

After she fed her, they both fell asleep, exhausted from their long night.

She woke up to the heavy sound of marching boots outside, and shouts in loud, angry German.

'*Schnell! Quick. Line up!*'

The guards were shouting for them to come outside. Her heart clenched in fear. Suddenly they were there.

'Everyone who is able to stand – move, outside, quickly!'

Acting fast, Helga and Sofie helped Eva wrap the baby in Eva's coat, and they left the baby on the top bunk.

'She will be safer here,' said Sofie.

Eva wasn't so sure. Leaving her behind felt like the hardest thing she had to do so far. But taking her could mean death if they saw her, or heard her.

Standing outside in the freezing cold, the snow heavy on the ground, was the longest two hours of her life. It wasn't an *Appell*. It was something else, something to do with the aeroplanes that were flying overhead. Finally, when an air raid sounded, the guard told them to return to their barracks, quickly. They scrambled. Eva was freezing cold in her thin dress, but all she could focus on was getting back to Naděje. Was she all right?

She raced back inside, on weak frozen limbs and hurtled into the top bunk, her shaking hands finding the tiny little bundle undisturbed. A small, perfect hand by her mouth, her cheeks faintly pink. Alive. Eva breathed out, fighting against a sudden bought of nausea from the fear.

She clutched her tiny newborn to her chest, rocking her and feeding her moments later, unbearably grateful that she could at least offer that to her child.

But the relief was short-lived. Throughout that cold, long day, the guards kept coming back, kept shouting at them to come outside and line up, and just as quickly the air raid would begin again and they would have to return, cold and shaken, to their bunks. After the third time, the guards stopped coming inside to call them out, and Eva decided to risk staying behind in the bunk, with the baby. Many of the sick, elderly and frail had chosen to wait inside too.

As the days passed, Eva tried her best to hide the baby from the others, it was easier now that the work units had stopped, and with it being so cold, no one ventured much past their bunks apart from going to the latrine or to eat what tiny portions of rations were available to them. Hunger had become a real problem, it was harder than ever to get what they needed now.

One bleak January morning, the snow turning everything white outside, Eva shuffled back from the latrine to her bunk on weak legs, her eyes bleary from fatigue and worry. She'd left Naděje in the warm bunk, and she climbed up to the top bunk, tired, and weary, wanting only to climb inside, clasp her child to her chest, and go to sleep – to try to block out the hunger pains that were ripping through her, only to gasp in sudden, paralysing fear.

It was empty.

# THIRTY-ONE

Eva scrambled down from the bunk, her heart roaring in her ears, her eyes scanning the barracks, which had emptied out from all the raids; many of the women who'd been ordered to leave and had followed had never returned. Had she missed a march?

'Have you seen Sofie?' she begged one of the women in the bunk below. 'Or Helga – it's important—'

The woman looked up and pointed to the end of barracks. Towards Maria's room. 'The *Kapo* was sniffing around here, she took something from your bunk. I saw her.'

Eva saw spots before her eyes as she raced to the small room at the end of the barracks that was for the *Kapo*'s sole use. She found the Polish woman with her back towards her.

'What have you done! Where's my baby?' cried Eva.

Maria's eyes were cool as she turned around. Naděje was asleep in her arms, and Eva's body grew limp in relief.

The *Kapo* considered Eva, then sniffed. 'You really are a fool.'

'Give her to me!' Eva demanded, coming forward to snatch her out of the woman's arms if need be.

To her shock, Maria gave her the baby. An annoyed look on her face.

As Eva clutched Naděje to her, Maria's expression grew resigned as she stared at the tiny baby in Eva's arms. 'If I were you, I'd say my goodbyes now – she's small, weak. It's likely she will die soon anyway. If you want, I will do it – take her outside – leave her with the others—'

'The others?' repeated Eva. A prickle of fear made her eyes snap to the Polish woman's.

Maria crossed her arms over herself as she explained. 'The dead.'

'No!' shouted Eva, cradling Naděje to her chest, tears pouring from her eyes.

Maria made a sound of disbelief. 'Look at her, you fool, she's going to die anyway. I won't risk my life for it.' Her jaw tensed and her expression softened slightly. 'You shouldn't either – if the guards come back and find her – and find out that I didn't tell them about it, they'll kill all three of us anyway – me, you, and the child.'

Eva shook her head wildly, trying to scrub away the *Kapo*'s words. 'No, *please*, Maria, I beg you. Don't do this.'

Maria shook her head. 'I'm sorry, but I have to.'

'No, you don't, Maria! You're a mother, that's what I heard. Please, I can't bear to lose my child.'

Maria's mouth turned into a frown. 'They killed *my* daughter. I'm not a mother anymore.'

Eva's eyes beseeched hers. 'You're still a mother—' A tear fell heavy from her lashes, and she didn't bother to wipe it away, as Naděje fussed in her arms, waking up. She patted her child's back gently. 'You went through that – why would you want to make someone else do it too? Please, Maria. I can't save your child, but you can save mine.'

Maria looked at Naděje. Her eyes grew cold. 'I won't call them – but if they come here, I won't lie for you – I will tell them about her – no one tried to help me, so that's the best you can hope for from me.'

Eva blinked at the *Kapo*'s words, then backed out of the room, her expression bleak. She would kill Maria before she allowed her to betray Naděje to the guards.

She walked slowly on leaden feet to her bunk – it felt like she was on death row, like an inmate waiting for the executioner to arrive, come dusk. She clutched her baby to her chest, and climbed back into her bunk. She didn't tell Sofie what had happened. She couldn't. Her friend had risked so much already with Meier, with Geneva. She wouldn't put her in that position again.

Outside the air raids continued, and the sound of guns and shellfire sounded ever closer. The war was turning against the Germans, but not soon enough.

Two days later they heard the sound of hob-nailed boots outside their block. Eva's heart hammered loudly in her chest. They were back! She picked up Naděje, and hid her beneath her clothes, close to her chest. The baby squirmed, but lay still, quiet.

A second later they were inside. Women scrambled from their bunks in fear, in haste. Fear ripped through the room, leaving behind an acrid stench.

'*Schnell*, quickly, follow us!' shouted Hinterschloss at the entryway. Eva scrambled with the others, landing awkwardly with her small bundle crooked to her breast, so that she took the impact on her knees, wincing in pain.

His eyes scanned over the room quickly, pausing to look at her for a second, before he marched on, tapping women with his rifle and making them hurry up.

Eva quickly lined up with the others, as far away from him as she could, looking frantically for Maria. Would the *Kapo* betray her? Surely it was safer to keep quiet? She had to believe that and believe that somehow she could convince her of that. She could find no trace of her as they were led outside into the fallen snow.

Those who were frail or could not stand were left behind. They marched out into the frozen night, and they didn't stop even as their knees sunk into the thick snow. Eva's heart thudded in her chest – in the other raids that she and Sofie hadn't followed, many of the people who had left the barracks hadn't come back.

She couldn't help her fear as they were led down to a tunnel, following behind Sofie. The baby squirmed beneath her coat, and she soothed her with a gentle pat.

'Halt,' cried Hinterschloss, shining a flashlight in their faces, as he came to walk back down the line.

Eva's legs flooded with fear. He stood looking at them all for a while, his cold, grey eyes falling on hers for a moment, then moving on down the line.

'Carry on, walk!' he ordered, shoving one of the women so that she stumbled. The flashlight clicked off and Eva breathed out a sigh of relief, and followed, shifting the bundle in her arms slightly.

Suddenly she felt a hard hand clamp on her shoulder, and she smelt his foul breath before she saw him. She looked up in the dark tunnel, to find Hinterschloss's face inches from hers, his mouth twisting in an evil leer. Behind him she saw a flash of a frightened face, Maria. Eva felt as if she'd been doused in icy water. As angry and scared as she'd been, a part of her had naively believed that Maria wouldn't betray her, despite her words. The *Kapo* didn't meet her shocked eyes.

'Let's see what we have here,' he said, making a mad snatch for the baby in her arms. Eva wrenched her arm away, and he took out a pistol, looking over his shoulder at the *Kapo*. 'This one has been asking for it for a long time,' he said with a leer. 'Our little translator. Always putting herself in places she shouldn't – including spreading her legs.' He spat on the ground, then sneered at her. 'You filthy whore!'

He cocked the pistol. The sound was loud in the dark tunnel and there were sharp intakes of breath. His eyes flashed dangerously. 'I should have done this the day I met you.'

'No!' cried Sofie behind her.

Maria looked away, she had the grace not to meet Eva's eyes. 'I'm sorry,' she said, so softly Eva wasn't sure if she had imagined it.

'What's going on?' called Meier, down the snaking queue of women in the tunnel.

As Hinterschloss turned to answer, Eva made a sudden dive for the gun. Sofie scrambled to help her, and was pushed back. The pistol fell to the ground and both Eva and Hinterschloss dived for it. Eva's fingers were inches from it, but she was hindered by the baby in her arms, unlike the stronger, fitter guard, who kicked at her side, his hand closing over the pistol. Suddenly there was a loud crack and Hinterschloss slumped over, falling to his knees, blood pooling from his temple. Eva looked up, in shock, to see Sofie standing behind him with a rock in her arms.

There were cheers as the ragtail group of prisoners saw the guard lying face down in the dirt. But the cheers quickly turned to screams as the sound of a rifle blasted through the cold, dark air, leaving a smoky trail.

Eva watched in slow horror as her friend fell over, a look of shock and betrayal flitting on her face as she slid onto her knees, blood mushrooming out of her chest.

'No!' shouted Eva, racing forward to catch her friend. Maria followed, and was pushed back angrily by Helga, who screeched, 'Get away from her!' To everyone's surprise she stood back, a look of regret on her face.

Eva watched in agony as Sofie slumped forward, the life draining from her.

Helga stepped forward. 'Give me Naděje,' she whispered. Eva didn't respond, and the old woman prised the child out of her arms. She dipped her head to listen to the child's lungs, 'The child is fine,' she said, touching Eva's shoulder softly as Eva knelt before her friend, trying somehow to stem the flow of blood with her hands. She couldn't see for the tears in her eyes.

'Help her, please,' cried Eva, sobs wracking through her thin frame. She couldn't lose Sofie!

Meier stood frozen, a few metres away from where he'd shot the woman he'd claimed to love, a look of disbelief on his face. The rifle was still pointed in their direction.

Eva cradled her friend against her chest. Sofie's face was as pale as the snow outside, and a thin trickle of blood ribboned from her lips as she tried to speak. Eva wiped it away, 'You'll be okay, Sofie, you'll survive this,' she lied, she hoped.

Sofie's breathing was thin and ragged. 'I'll miss you, *Kritzelei*,' she said. 'Find Tomas for me.'

'We'll find him together, like we said,' cried Eva, holding on tightly, but Sofie's body was already limp in her arms, her dark eyes seeing no more. Eva howled, clutching her all the harder.

'G-get back to your hut,' commanded Meier. 'I will deal with the body.'

Eva launched herself at Meier, ready to tear him apart. Maria grabbed hold of her. The *Kapo* was strong, and resisted her even as Eva tried to attack her instead. 'Stop,' she hissed. 'You'll get yourself killed!'

'Which is what you wanted!' shouted Eva, but the *Kapo* just held on tight, not letting her go. Eva was weak, her body tiny and malnourished, no match for the well-fed *Kapo*.

After some time, Meier just shook his head. His blue eyes fell on Sofie's body. They were full of regret. He knelt down beside her, then picked up her hand, his own shaking as he lifted it to his face. He closed his eyes, and shook his head. 'I didn't want to do this,' he whispered. He looked like he'd aged ten years in the space of seconds. He glanced up, and there was moisture in his blue eyes, as he gave Maria an order.

'Take Eva away. The baby can stay with her. It will die soon anyway.' Then, very softly, as he turned back to touch Sofie's face, closing her eyes, they heard him say, 'It's what she would have wanted.'

The *Kapo* nodded. As she frogmarched Eva back to the barracks, she whispered, 'It's your lucky day.'

Eva managed to get one hand free enough to strike the *Kapo* across her face. She paid for it with a punch in return, and saw only black stars afterwards, as she passed out.

\*

A few of the other women half carried her back to the barracks – they were sick and frail, and it took far longer than it normally would. Helga carried her tiny charge safe in her arms, cradling her to her chest. Naděje had fallen asleep, oblivious to the horror surrounding her. Helga touched her little face with a gnarled finger. It was for the best. One of the other women looked at the baby in the old woman's arms and shook her head. 'Poor girl, all of that over a doll.'

She wouldn't believe that the tiny bundle was a real baby.

*

When Eva came round, she was in the top bunk again with the other women, Naděje in a blanket beside her. Her head was splitting in pain from where Maria had punched her, but all she could do was gasp from the ache in her heart when she remembered what had happened.

Helga passed her a wedge of black bread, and she ate it with unseeing eyes for her daughter's sake, thanking the old woman for her kindness. Helga patted her back. She didn't offer empty condolences, didn't pretend that things would be better in time, and Eva was grateful for that.

As the days passed in a sea of grief, there were shouts for them to come outside. Once again those who were able to walk were told to come. '*Schnell*. Quickly.'

Hundreds of prisoners scrambled outside into the freezing cold to begin what would be known later as the death marches.

The sick and the elderly stayed behind. Once again, Eva watched as no guards came inside to drag them out; she held

Naděje to her chest, closed her eyes, and blew out her cheeks. Next to her Helga said, 'You aren't going to go?'

Eva shook her head. The last time she'd left they'd almost died.

Helga nodded. The old woman's eyes were wide with fear. She was thin, frail, tired too. She nodded.

No one came inside to check. Perhaps the guards figured they would die soon enough in their beds without food. It was likely. They'd finished the last of the bread.

They watched the others leave. It turned out to be a momentous decision.

# THIRTY-TWO

They awoke to quiet. No dogs barked. No jackboots marched outside. The background hum of thousands of human beings clinging onto their lives was gone.

It was just quiet. An odd stillness that she hadn't heard in months, if not years. The barracks was nearly empty, the only ones left behind were skeletal shapes, close to death.

Helga came back from the outside, shuffling into the bunk, her eyes wide. 'They're gone,' she breathed.

'Gone?' whispered Eva, getting out of the bunk, Naděje close to her breast, needing to check for herself. Eva wrapped a thin jacket over them, and made her way outside to stare.

There was no one there.

No floodlights lit up the camp. No booted feet marched. The guard towers were empty. They'd been abandoned to their fate.

Knowing that the Germans had gone felt like the first ray of sun in the longest winter. She looked down at her tiny baby, still miraculously alive despite her size, her weak lungs still unable to make more than a thin gurgling sound, and kissed her smooth cheek. A tear, this time of surprise and joy mixed with regret, rolled down her cheek.

She missed her friend, more now than ever. 'Oh Sofie, just a few more days, and we would have been free, together.'

She looked up, past the fence, and for the first time, saw beyond it, and vowed, 'I will find him, your Tomas, like I promised you. I will raise him – I will raise our children together.'

Those who had been left behind were close to death. Even though their tormentors had finally left, survival would be harder than ever. Soviet planes had bombed the nearby factory and there was no electricity or water. Those who could walk – like Eva – would need to call on their very last reserves to keep going, to keep fighting. It seemed incredibly cruel as so many of the people who had clung on to life now began to die.

Eva was surprised to find that Maria was one of the left behind. She had grown pale and weak in a short space of time, and the change was shocking. Eva suspected she was suffering from Typhus. The Kapo stayed in her room, and they left her to it.

She looked at Helga and said, 'It's not over yet. We're going to have to be strong. Find food. Clothes. Water.'

Helga nodded. 'And carry out the dead.'

Which was the worst part, having to move the bodies of the people who died in the night, and there were many.

\*

Together they broke into the Kanada and found piles of clean clothing, decent shoes, socks and blankets. For the first time in years she had proper boots that kept her feet warm. The feeling was delicious.

They brought back blankets and clothes and shared these with all they could.

At first to slake their thirst they melted snow, but soon hacked up ice from a nearby frozen pond by the gates. It was hard work and it took its toll.

Maria lay sick, near death still in her private room. She'd protested when the others had begun to take her things, using up the last of her supplies, but she'd been too weak to prevent them.

Looking at her lying weak and pale on the bed, feverish, Eva couldn't help but feel that maybe she'd been paid back for her betrayal.

When she came inside the room to fetch a bucket, her thin cry made her turn. 'Eva, please. I need medicine. It's typhus, I think. Please, Eva. Please remember that I helped you.'

Eva turned to look at her, a frown between her eyes. 'You helped me?'

'Yes – that's how you have your child, because I turned my back so you could see your husband. You can hate me if you want but if it weren't for me—' She stopped and started to cough, wheezing as she fell back against the thin mattress.

'Yes, you did do that. But only because you were well paid.' The *Kapo* had been given parcels of food that Sofie and Eva had managed to scrounge, and even then when she'd taken the food she'd made no promises that she would protect her, just keep her mouth shut. She hadn't even kept that promise in the end, had she? And it had led to her best friend's death. 'Please, Eva, I'll die if someone doesn't help me.'

Eva clenched her jaw. 'Yes,' and she turned on her heel to leave, saying over her shoulder, 'That's the case for all of us.'

With two of the other stronger women, they broke into a storeroom in the kitchen and were amazed to find row upon row of black bread, as well as cheese and jam. Putting them in heavy sack bags, they dragged their goods back to the barracks, and those who could feasted on more food than they had in years.

Eva's stomach was so small that she was full just after two slices, but she crammed in a thick wedge of cheese for good measure, thinking wryly that the dairy might ensure that her milk continued to flow as Naděje suckled on her small breast, her tiny hand near Eva's heart. 'That's it, baby,' she said. 'We'll get strong together.'

'Where are you going?' asked Helga as Eva sat on the edge of the bunk, her legs dangling on the ground. She made her decision, then handed Naděje to the old woman and got to her feet.

'I'll be back soon.'

Her hands reached into the pocket of the thick, cosy coat she'd found at the Kanada with its fur collar, and she straightened her spine as she walked to the end towards the *Kapo*'s room.

'Here,' she said, handing her two wedges of bread and a bottle of antibiotics they'd found in their scrummage of the warehouse.

Maria tried to sit up, and Eva reluctantly came forward to help her. 'Thank you,' said Maria, opening the pill bottle and swallowing one. It seemed to take a long time as she was very weak.

'I'm sorry about your friend,' she said at last. 'I liked her. I never meant for that to happen.'

Eva nodded, dashing away a tear. She got up to leave and Maria said, 'She would be glad that you helped me.'

Eva turned back to look at her and scoffed, a trace of humour about her lips. 'No, she wouldn't. She would have said, *'Kritzelei, you're a fool, she almost got you killed.'*

Maria blinked. 'Why then?'

'Because I'll never be able to forgive you for causing her death, but at least I won't have yours on my conscience now.'

# THIRTY-THREE

Eva woke to the sound of armoured cars and tanks and then shouting and gun shots.

'Wake up,' she hissed to Helga. 'We need to hide.'

Six days after they had left, the Germans returned.

Helga looked at her, her eyes wide, her lank hair seemed to crackle with fear. 'They've come back to finish us off!'

'Maybe,' said Eva. 'I won't let that happen.'

They crept outside, but fell back when they saw, in the distance, guards marching. In the snow there were fresh bodies, and they saw Maria stagger slowly past them, outside.

'Come back, don't be a fool!' called Eva. But the former *Kapo* walked on bare feet through the thick drifts. Her clothing hung off her like a sack – she'd lost a lot of weight in recent weeks, a combination of her illness and the loss of her favoured position with the guards. She staggered, possibly delirious, trying to call the guards who were some distance ahead. Her thin cracked lips, crying out, 'Help me.'

One of them turned. A shot rang out and Maria sank backwards into a pool of blood turning pink in the fresh snow.

Eva and Helga stifled a gasp. The guards carried on walking, not bothering to look back, shooting any stray prisoners they encountered with impunity. Eva and Helga huddled just beyond the doorway, out of sight.

In the distance, there was the sound of an explosion.

'They're blowing up the other crematoria,' guessed Helga.

They watched in shock as the Germans got back into their armoured cars and left.

'Do you think they will come back?' she asked.

Eva looked at her, clutching her baby to her chest. Her eye fell on Maria's body, growing cold in the snow. 'I don't know.'

They'd had a lucky escape but they were stuck here. The Germans may have left Auschwitz but they were still fighting the Soviets nearby. The war wasn't over yet and until that happened, they dare not risk leaving.

Two days later, as Helga and two of the other women were walking to get more ice from the pond, heavy buckets in their arms, they saw what looked like a bear at the gates.

Eva blinked as more and more of them began to appear. Finally, she realised that they were men, in large overcoats.

'It's the Russians!' shouted one of the women, whooping in joy. 'They've come to set us free!'

*

Eva watched as they made their way into the camp, greeting the women who fell upon them crying and hugging them in their joy. They were civil, and courteous, which after years of brutality felt like kindness.

One of the men – who had a long thin scar running down his face, just below his left eye, and startling blue eyes – looked at her and said in broken German, 'When we came through here I thought you were all ghosts.'

Soon there were warm fires burning and the men invited them to warm themselves by the flames. They shared their food readily too. Not realising that this kindness would be the undoing of some of these poor women, their bodies so starved and malnourished their systems didn't know how to cope with an overload of fat; many ended up dying from diarrhoea as they couldn't process the new diet.

Eva watched in horror as more and more women in their barracks got sick, complaining of stomach cramps, their wasted bodies giving up on them when they were now so close to freedom. 'Don't eat their food,' she told Helga. 'No matter how much we want to – I think it's making us sick. Just stick to the bread and cheese.'

'*Kritzelei*,' complained Helga. 'You can't think they're poisoning us – we're eating the same food as them.'

For Eva, having her still be called Sofie's nickname, was both a comfort, and a torment. 'Not poison, just too rich maybe.'

Helga nodded. They'd watched too many die. She would be careful.

\*

The man with the scar kept coming back inside the barracks, wanting to chat with the women. He was curious about the survivors. It was hard for them all to explain what had happened. To talk about what the Germans had done. He seemed most interested in the baby. 'Was it – one of theirs?' he asked, not unkindly.

Eva shook her head. 'No, it was my husband's. We found each other, here.'

He looked at her, his blue eyes solemn. 'Well, that is the first good thing I have heard about this place. I'm glad.'

She nodded.

'I am Stanislav,' he said introducing himself. She looked at him carefully and then stuck out her hand. 'Eva.'

Stanislav and their liberators were soldiers from the 60th army of the 1st Ukrainian Front. He'd grown up in Odessa, a beautiful city on the Black Sea, so he said. He was married, with two young sons, but back home he used to be a professor of literature. 'It's not much use here. But I tell the men poetry sometimes.'

'Does it help?'

He inclined his head. 'Sometimes.'

She looked up at him and said, 'Tennyson, "The Charge of the Light Brigade". An English poem I learnt at school – my

238

father wanted me to learn the language,' she explained, feeling a twinge of pain as she thought of him, and her family, of her old life, when such things had seemed to matter. 'That's as much as I know of the Ukraine.'

He frowned. 'I don't know that one,' he said with a frown. She recited the poem about the needless killing of six hundred men who were ordered to fight, even though they were facing certain death by a foolish commander in the Battle of Balaclava in the Crimean War in 1854, '… *Someone had blundered. Theirs not to make reply, theirs not to reason why. Theirs but to do and die, into the valley of Death, rode the six hundred…*'

Eva couldn't help thinking that the Germans had followed a madman in the same way.

Until this war was over, they were like those 600, waiting and hoping that their new guardians would lead them towards victory, towards freedom at long last.

# THIRTY-FOUR

Helga and Eva managed to find a room away from the barracks, and they spent their first night in years in real beds.

As they regained some strength they began to look forward, to think of how they might rebuild their lives. Eva had one thought only and that was to get back to Prague. To find out what happened to her family. After that she would keep her promise to Sofie, she would find Tomas, somehow.

For Helga, freedom came at a hard price. There was no one left in her family. 'They're all dead,' she said, tears in her eyes. 'My parents died when I was a little girl. I was an only child. My husband was my life, and my two sons, and I watched as they got shot – the day I arrived here. It's why I almost gave up. There's no one.'

Eva reached out and clutched her hand. 'You've got me.'

Helga looked at her. 'I can't go live with you.'

'Why not?'

'Because – your family—?'

'Helga, we've been sleeping next to each other for two years. You are my family now.'

The old woman dashed a tear from her eyes, and touched Naděje's little hand and nodded.

Some of the other women wanted to go to Auschwitz I to see if the men were alive – many of the Soviet soldiers were going there as well, and it was thought it would be safer than Birkenau in case the Germans came back. It was a long, interminable walk through the snow, and Eva had to help Helga get through it. She was stronger now, but they were all painfully thin, and weak, even with more food in their bellies, it would take many of them years before they would fully recover, if they ever truly did. Their bodies might, but their lives would forever be changed. They were not the same people they'd arrived here as. At twenty-six, Eva felt like an old woman.

When they arrived at Auschwitz I, the remaining men were overjoyed to see them. They welcomed them warmly. In the crowd, Eva found Herman and they embraced for a long time. 'Oh, I'm so glad to see you're alive,' he cried.

'Not just me,' she said, and showed him the baby that he'd had a small part in bringing into the world. His mouth fell open.

'Is that Michal's?'

She nodded and the old man stared down at the baby, as the men around them spoke to the other women, asking after their wives. Some were crying, many were sharing warm smiles.

Eva and Helga slept in an old *Kapo*'s room in the men's barracks.

Herman came to visit often, bringing whatever food he could. 'You have always been so generous, thank you,' she said as she ate the salami he offered.

'It's from the Russians,' he said.

They watched the Soviets warily. The truth was their lives were in these men's hands. They felt like they could trust them, but after everything they'd been through they couldn't be sure who or what to trust ever again.

On their third evening in the new camp, Eva passed Stanislav who was sitting by a fire. He held his hands out towards the flames. 'Eva,' he called, and she stopped. 'Would you like a coffee?'

Eva cradled Naděje to her chest. Her baby was still far too small, but she had grown slightly, and seemed stronger. She had yet to cry properly though, beyond short gurgling wheezes, her tiny lungs were just too weak.

'That would be nice, thank you.'

She watched as he put a tin kettle onto the coals, then spooned freshly ground coffee into the pot. She sighed in pleasure as the rich aroma permeated the smoky air.

'It's been several years since I tasted the real thing,' she said.

He nodded. 'I can imagine, you've been away from the outside world for a long time.' The firelight fell on the scars on his face, and his blue gaze turned towards her. 'I was thinking of that when you walked past actually. You will need a birth certificate for your child. I can take you to the town tomorrow.'

Eva blinked. A birth certificate. 'From here?'

'You will need it.'

Eva stared down at Naděje. 'Born in Auschwitz, that's some legacy.'

Stanislav was true to his word and in the morning, she travelled with him and Helga to the town. 'We must be careful – the Germans have left the camp but they are still around in the town. Stay close to me,' he said, patting his rifle.

They made their way into the small courthouse, the sight of the Ukrainian soldier causing more than a little unease as a group of clerks dropped their files as soon as they entered.

'What is going on? We don't have anything for you!' cried one of the men.

'We don't want any trouble,' said Helga. The man sneered, and Stanislav frowned.

'We need a birth certificate.'

'We can't do that – not without—'

Stanislav stepped forward. 'This child was born in that camp – which you allowed to continue for years – acknowledging that is the least you can do.'

He stared from the tall, bearded man to the skeletal frames of Helga and Eva, and the tiny baby in her arms, and nodded. 'We don't want any trouble – come with me.'

Eva left with a signed birth certificate, with Naděje's birth listed as 6 January 1945. Officially she was Naděje Sofie Adami, and her place of birth was Oświęcim. She looked at it and frowned. 'It should say Auschwitz,' she said, 'but the clerk said that it wasn't an official place. Neither is hell, but we all know what it is.'

# THIRTY-FIVE

They listened in fear all night long to the crack of gunfire and the heavy boom of the artillery. In the early hours of the morning, Stanislav entered their barracks. The soldier was dressed in his heavy overcoat, a grim set to his lips. 'We think it will be safer to take you all behind Soviet lines. The Germans are edging back towards us. We believe they may try to blow this place up. We're leaving today.'

Eva and Helga shared looks of fear. Neither of them wanted to die now – not when they were so close to finally getting out of here.

They gathered together their meagre possessions, and with the other survivors walked out in to the cold February dawn. Many would walk, while some were carried by Soviet trucks to the station. From Birkenau, they would find out later that more than a million Jews had died, and only six thousand survived. Naděje opened her eyes as the cold gathered ground as they marched on, with the long snaking line of survivors. Then she closed them again, burying her face against Eva's chest, not seeing as the mist swirled, and Auschwitz was swallowed behind them in the fog.

Eva clutched Helga's hand and the two drew strength from each other, with one last look over their shoulders. She couldn't believe the day had finally come. They were leaving at last.

*

What should have been a simple trip of a matter of hours would actually take weeks. Much of the railway had been shelled in bombings, and Eva and Helga boarded the same cattle trains that had taken them to Auschwitz. Except that this time, they were given food and there were frequent stops. As they passed further into Poland, they saw whole villages that had been wiped out, people living in makeshift shelters. The war hadn't been kind to them either.

They survived on the benevolence of the Russian soldiers, and had to be careful to stick together. Travelling further into Poland, when they finally reached the city of Katowice, Eva couldn't help agonising that it was the opposite of where they wanted to be, going further east when her heart wanted to lead them home. They were given lodgings, and spent the night in their first proper rooms.

Helga turned to her and smiled, her hair fresh and clean in new clothes, and said, 'I feel almost normal.'

*

On their first morning in the city, Eva had new worries, cradling Naděje to her chest. Her baby's cheeks were red, and her face was screwed up tight. 'I think she's got a fever,' said Helga, feeling her forehead.

They shared worried looks, and Eva stood up to get her coat. 'We'll have to go to the hospital.'

They walked past smart shops and streets to the hospital, but Eva didn't take in any of the sights – with each breath she worried over her daughter's fate.

In a mix of German and Czech she was able to explain to one of the nurses what was wrong, and shortly afterwards a Ukrainian paediatrician, named Anna Zagorsky, with a pretty face, and short black hair, called them into her office, watching them approach with concerned eyes.

Eva tried as best as she could to explain what in years to come would remain inexplicable. News had travelled, of course, about Auschwitz, but it would take years for people to fully appreciate what had occurred there. For most, the scale of the Nazis' cruelty and vile ideology was so far removed from normal life that it was hard to imagine. Even here, now, with a country at war. But it was the nurses and doctors who tried their best to look after the survivors who were the ones faced with it first.

Anna Zogorsky looked at Naděje with pity in her eyes.

'She is very small,' she said, looking her over. 'Weak, especially her bones, which is probably due to the malnutrition,' she said, looking up at Eva's tiny frame.

Eva nodded. 'Will she be all right?'

The doctor listened to her chest, and examined her some more. 'She's fighting an infection, I think. I will need to run some tests to see what it is. I'm concerned about her lungs. She hasn't cried yet?'

Eva shook her head. 'Small noises, but no real crying.'

Anna nodded. 'I think it would be best if the three of you—' her eye darted from Eva to Helga who was standing silently, like an old crow, by the door, watching over her chicks, 'stayed here for a while. I'm going to need to keep her under observation.' Then her eyes met Eva's and answered her question, making Eva's heart clench. 'We can only hope. She's got this far, I think she might – she seems tough, like her mother,' she said, laying her hand on hers for a moment. Eva couldn't help thinking that if she was tough, it was only because of Sofie, because of what her friend had done for her. She closed her eyes in pain, grief. Missing her was a constant ache.

Eva, Helga and Naděje stayed in hospital for over two months. As soon as they had stopped moving, stopped travelling, it was as if their starved, malnourished bodies broke down, and they spent the next few weeks in bed, struck down with pneumonia. It was agony for Eva to be separated from her child – worse still as, a result of her illness, her milk dried up. The nurses, thankfully, had powdered formula that they had received from

America via the Red Cross. Eva was lucky to have found her way here. Baby formula wasn't easy to come by in such times.

Anna, however, was reassuring, as she sat on the edge of her bed and gave her an update on her daughter's condition. 'She is a fighter if ever I saw one. She's responded well to the antibiotics, and as soon as you're better we can bring her to stay with you. Eva, I must tell you though that it will be tough for her – I'm not sure if she will be able to walk – not for many years at least, her bones are very weak.'

Eva looked at the kind doctor, and said, 'But she will have those years now, thank you.'

It would be a long road to recovery, as Eva and Helga's thin bodies battled with pneumonia, using up what little reserves they had left. All that was left to do was sleep, which was a luxury that they embraced. Despite her age, Helga seemed to recover faster. 'You drove yourself hard, trying to stay alive for all of us – breaking into storerooms, hacking away at the ice, I think it took its toll harder,' was Helga's reasoning.

Whatever the case, Eva was grateful that Helga pulled through. She didn't know if she could face being alone, face losing another loved one.

Her dreams were a relief, and a torment. Her brain kept putting her back in Auschwitz, no matter how much further they were from ever having to set foot there again. Some nights she dreamt that she found Michal again in that storeroom where they'd made love – his face would be covered in bruises, but she could still see his green eyes, that soft dimple, still feel the warmth of his arms as she fitted herself against his chest. She would wake with tears in her eyes, wishing for just one more day, one more moment with him.

At other times, she writhed in terror, smelling Hinterschloss's foul, whisky-soaked breath, before she saw him. Those grey eyes, the whites turned yellow, narrowing as he pointed a pistol at her and fired in the dark tunnel, somehow it was always him who shot her friend. In the day she would wake, leaving the darkness behind, and her terror, in the delight of her baby's soft cheeks, and warm body next to hers. She couldn't help, when she dreamt of Michal or Sofie, how happy she was to see them again, even if it meant crossing back into hell to do so.

As her body began to recover, and Naděje grew stronger from the combined force of Eva's will, formula milk, and the paediatrician's care, Eva dreamt that her friend was shaking her awake. She turned, and saw her sitting on the edge of her hospital bed, her long, dark blonde hair fresh and clean, and falling over her shoulder, her dark eyes warm, a surprised smile on her lips, as she whispered her secret into Eva's ear. '*Kritzelei*, the Germans have surrendered.'

When she woke up with a start, her eye fell on the small cot they had placed near her bed as Anna had promised. Eva stared down at her daughter, who screwed up a fist, and from her lips came the smallest thinnest cry. Eva blinked back the tears. It was the first cry she'd made since she was born.

In the hospital halls, the news swelled, thrumming along the walls, and Eva and Helga turned to one another as someone shouted, 'It's over, it's finally over – they have surrendered!'

# THIRTY-SIX

There was a whisper of summer when they finally made their way into Prague, after weeks of travelling. The Soviets had helped them, given them clothes and food, and arranged their transport.

It was all Eva could think about: home. Her mind had filled with thoughts of her beloved city. Her family, her small apartment. Were any of them still alive?

Against Anna's and the hospital's wishes, Eva and Helga had decided to leave. Naděje was stronger now – stronger than she'd ever been, as was Helga. 'I still think you should stay, rest – you're a bit better, Eva, but you're at a big risk of relapse if you go now. Your body has been through a lot – give it time.'

Eva had touched Anna's hand. 'I can't thank you enough for your care, truly, but I need to go home, I need to find out what happened to the rest of my family. Find my friend's son. Then I can rest.'

The doctor gave her a hug. 'Just promise me you'll take care of yourself.'

'I will, thank you again.'

*

She would never forget that first sight of her city, as they disembarked from the train. The sun was warm on their shoulders, and for the first time in years they were on their own. It was both wondrous and overwhelming, after having their every moment controlled by others for so long – the sheer freedom that stretched before them was terrifying. Eva was so thankful that Helga was with her as they saw their first glimpse of Prague, and Eva felt her own home ground beneath her feet. After wishing and praying she would see it again, it felt foreign. The city was relatively unscathed compared to many of the towns and villages they had passed, many of which had been reduced to rubble, but it had been bombed, the worst of which had occurred in February of that year, when 152 tons of bombs were dropped on populated areas, killing over a thousand people. Compared to other cities though, the damage wasn't as severe, despite the fact that many lost their homes. As Eva and Helga disembarked, she couldn't help noting the change, and everywhere she looked it was as if they were surrounded by ghosts.

They were greeted warmly by many of the residents, many of whom offered them food – though some had their own worries: they had suffered greatly too under the Germans, having been forcibly expelled after a mass uprising weeks before liberation. While some offered them what little they had, others turned them away, they had had their fill of suffering.

Eva didn't take much notice of the reaction of the city's population, she was in a rush to go to her parents' apartment to see if anyone was there. In the square, officials had set up vast noticeboards for the survivors, so they could look for their loved ones. Eva and Helga scanned these, their eyes filling as they didn't recognise anyone they knew.

'They might just be at the apartment, waiting for me,' said Eva, still hopeful after all this time.

Helga didn't say that it was unlikely. She didn't need to. The faces of the people they passed said enough.

\*

When Eva got to her parents' apartment, her knees dropped out from under her, and Helga had to catch her before she fell to the ground. The building was gone, reduced to a pile of rubble. As she sobbed, Helga holding on to Naděje, Eva combed through the detritus, looking for anything that she could salvage. In the wreckage, she came across shoes, and scattered documents, an old leather file caught her eye, buried under grey dust. She wiped it with her palms, and opened it. Her heart caught in her throat. It was sheet music, Michal's.

Helga had to help her stand, then they staggered on through the night, asking blindly, not sure of where to go, where to turn. She passed by her old apartment, which had been her first home with Michal, before they were asked to leave, and saw a young couple with a child walking up the steps. Her eye was drawn to the window, where she'd once laid a peach for Michal as an offering for the beautiful music that had captured her heart on the streets below.

Through the lighted window, Eva's heart clenched to see that the same green and blue rug adorned the floor which had been worn bare from Michal's old shoes while he played.

Did the couple who lived there now hear the whisper of the music in the walls, the echo from their old lives? Did they think of the people who once made that apartment their home, as they held their child?

She turned away from the happy couple, with their small son, seeing three pairs of feet as they crossed by the window, trying to drive away the thought that they hadn't just taken their home, but their future too.

# THIRTY-SEVEN

Eva had dreamt so long of returning home, but without her family and their apartment, it didn't feel like home anymore. The city was full of broken people trying to return to something they couldn't.

She walked the old city with Naděje in her arms, drawing strength from her. She had her daughter, she reminded herself, and that was reason enough to keep going, to keep moving. As dawn broke, Eva turned to her friend. 'There's one other place we can try. My family's summer home. I'm not sure if they would have gone there – at this point I'm not sure of anything really.'

Helga nodded, her dark eyes full. 'It's worth trying. What else are we going to do? It's not like we can stay here.'

Eva looked up, past the river she'd longed to see for so long, the castle winking in the apricot light, and admitted the truth. 'No, there's nothing here for us now.'

They had one thing to do before they left.

They made their way back to the square, to the noticeboards, and Eva and Helga put down their names, with the note of where they would be. It was weeks since liberation, it had taken Eva and Helga a long time to make their way here, by now surely the others would be here – if they had survived.

She put her name down anyway. 'Oh, *Kritzelei*,' said Helga, but it wasn't an admonishment, not really.

\*

With what little money they had been given from the authorities when they arrived, she boarded a train, and headed for *Jívka* in the *Hradec Králové* region. On the journey Eva grew ill, and couldn't stop coughing. Helga felt her forehead, her eyes worried, and took Naděje from her, giving the baby her bottle, which they'd prepared in the early hours of the morning in the station.

'I'm worried about you, you heard what the doctor said,' whispered Helga.

Eva shook her head, which was foggy, her brain clouded. She felt weak and tired. 'I'll be all right, we just need to keep going. I'll rest when we're there.'

'It's the stress – it must have been,' said Helga, referring to the bombed-out apartment, the empty city's streets.

Eva didn't deny it. Just repeated the words like a mantra. 'I'll be all right.'

They made it to the summer house, and Eva caught sight of the red-roofed building along the mountainside. She got as far as the drive and had to sit.

'I'll just rest here a little while,' she told Helga, her eyes starting to close.

'Come on,' said Helga, 'it's not that far,' she lied.

Eva's eyelashes fluttered, and a deep cough wracked through her body. Naděje's eyes screwed up and she started to make a thin gurgling sound, it was her form of crying.

Eva looked up, in the distance she could see someone running towards them but before she could lift her head to see, she'd passed out.

When she woke up, she saw her old housekeeper's face. 'Oh, *dítě*,' she cried, seeing her awake. 'I can't believe you're alive.'

Eva started to cry. Kaja was the closest thing to family she'd seen in years. The older woman gathered her to her chest.

Eva's eyes scanned the room. 'The baby is with your friend, Helga,' said Kaja, touching her arm gently. Eva nodded, her eyes searching.

'It's just us, no one else has returned.'

Eva's lips trembled, and she nodded. A hand coming up to cover her mouth.

'I'm sorry,' said Kaja, not knowing what else to say.

As the days passed, Helga and Kaja became friends, and Eva slowly recovered from her relapse. The old housekeeper told her own story of having to hide away from the Germans, after her home was taken away. 'As you know, I normally only come here for the summers, but there was nowhere else to go.'

Eva reached out a hand, 'I'm so glad you did. This is your home too.'


The doctors in Katowice had warned them not to eat too much rich food, to keep their diets plain, and it was hard to convince Kaja and themselves not to cook everything they had missed – hot roasted potatoes, rich summer stews and soups, but she kept the fare simple as directed. Even so, despite meagre rations from a country still recovering from war, they slowly began to heal, and Eva started to make plans for getting to Austria to find Tomas, within weeks of their return to *Jívka*.

Kaja and Helga were against it. 'You're still weak,' said Kaja, 'it can wait a while, stay, swim in the lake, recover, feel the sun on your shoulders. God knows you've earned it, after all you've been through.'

Eva shook her head. 'It's been months already since we left Auschwitz – far too long. I need to find him, who knows where they might send him now that there's no word of her return? I made a promise to my friend.'

'She would understand if you took some time to recuperate, gather your strength.'

Eva shook her head, denying it. 'She wouldn't – she risked her life for my child. What kind of a friend am I if I won't do the same?'

'She wanted you to raise her child, you can't do that if you're dead,' pointed out Helga in a huff by the door, Naděje in the old woman's arms. Her skin had started to turn brown, and there was a bit more flesh on her bones. Her hair was almost completely white, yet she looked healthier than she had in years.

'I'll be all right,' said Eva.

Helga rolled her eyes, patting the baby's back, as she shook her head at Eva. 'You always say that, *Kritzelei*, and then you never are,' she huffed.

The child's arms reached out for her mother who snuggled her close to her chest, breathing in her warm, clean scent, marvelling once again at the joy she could bring to her broken heart.

Eva looked over her child's dark head: her hair was starting to grow, and it was beginning to curl, as she'd suspected it would, like her father's. She couldn't deny that. 'This time though, I think it's true.'

Eva had resisted at first, but had eventually given in to Helga and Kaja's argument that if she insisted on going to Austria now, it would be prudent to leave Naděje with them.

'She will be better off here with us. Who knows how long it will take to find him? It might be weeks, if not months. With a baby to worry about, there's a danger you could get ill again,' said Helga, her dark eyes firm. 'You're not fully recovered even now, no matter how much you insist.'

With trembling lips, she kissed Naděje goodbye. 'I'm going to fetch your brother,' she promised her. 'After that we can begin properly to be a family.' She looked up at the two older women, her adopted mothers, and smiled. 'We will need a boy around the house.'

Kaja smiled. 'That would be nice. I hope you find him, *dítě*.'

All Eva had to go on was the name of the town, on the westernmost point of Austria, Bregenz. A beautiful town, nestled between Lake Constance and the foothills of the Alps. Even here, so far out, in this wonderful spot, it was clear to see that the ravages of war had left their mark, as many of the homes had been destroyed by bombs.

It had taken several weeks to get to this point. With thousands of people leaving their homes, and immigrating to what they hoped would be more welcoming pockets of the world, travel was harder than ever, and getting the necessary documentation had proved a bothersome delay. But at last, Eva was here now. Every time she saw a woman with long, dark blonde hair, she felt as if she saw the ghost of her friend's smile, her determined stride, only to have the image vanish in an instant and a stranger look at her as if she were mad. She supposed, a few months out of Auschwitz, it still showed.

She found accommodation in a small hotel, and set about trying to locate Lotte's home. Here she discovered, like so many other towns, that all the Jews had been forcefully removed, and no neighbours could offer any advice or assistance. An old woman, who was walking alongside the bombed-out wreckage of her garage, hissed at her. 'I don't have anything for you, I have my own troubles,' she snapped, before going into the house and slamming the door behind her, mistakenly thinking that Eva was asking for a hand-out.

She'd tried the local Catholic church but had been turned away, there were no children there, and never had been, so they said.

She would need to look into nearby orphanages. But several of them had moved during the war.

She was fortunate enough to pass a local postman on his rounds, who recognised the name of the woman who'd helped deliver Tomas, Liesl, supplying her with a surname too. 'Must be the Streimers, she's the closest midwife,' he'd said when she asked. Hope blossomed in her chest. It felt like a real lead at last. Sofie had suggested it was possible that Liesl might know something about where Lotte had taken her son.

Eva found the house, down a dirt track, that had views of the lake. It was somewhat ramshackle, but pretty, and there were several children running in the yard, a tangle of limbs as they raced an old dog with caramel-coloured fur.

Eva paused as she saw one of the children, a little boy, with dirty blond hair, look back at her. She couldn't see his face clearly from where he stood. But there was something about the way he tilted his neck, his long limbs, that seemed familiar. He wasn't running with the others, or playing, he hung back then turned around and headed in the opposite direction, alone.

Eva stared. It couldn't be him, could it? After this long journey, she was sure she was just seeing Sofie's face in everyone.

There was a sound behind her, and Eva turned to find a plump woman with curly black hair standing by the front door. She was wearing an apron and a wary expression. 'Can I help you?' she asked, not unkindly. 'I don't have much – but there is some fresh bread and cheese I can offer you.'

Eva shook her head. 'No, thank you, that's kind. I'm here to see someone – Liesl?'

'That's me,' nodded the woman, her eyes narrowing. A practised eye fell on Eva's body, as if looking for a sign of pregnancy.

'You delivered my friend's child, Sofie.'

'I've helped deliver many children.'

Eva nodded. It figured she wouldn't make it easy. 'Her name was Sofie Weis.'

Liesl's eyes clouded, and she closed them for a moment, noting the past tense. 'Tomas's mother.'

Eva nodded. 'I need to find him.'

Liesl stared at her for a long moment and said, 'You'd better come inside.'

*

Liesl offered her a cup of tea, but she was too anxious for anything besides water. She waited as the other woman prepared a mug for herself, her hands busy as she put a kettle on the stove. The two little girls and the dog she'd seen outside raced indoors wanting to know who the skinny lady was, and Liesl shooed them out, with biscuits pressed into their palms, admonishing them for their rudeness.

'I'm sorry about that,' she said, taking a seat across from her at the worn kitchen table, which was covered in bread flour. 'And for earlier – I thought you were one of the others, you know…'

'Others?'

'They're calling them displaced persons – refugees, the ones who have lost their homes – the government have set up a small area for them, they don't have anywhere else to go for now. Sometimes we find some of them, thin and half-starved, looking for food.'

Eva nodded. She didn't feel much different to them, not really. She'd been just the same only a few short weeks ago.

Eva was impatient for news. If Liesl didn't know anything, then she would need to keep going. Begin the long task of knocking down every orphanage or nunnery door in the area in her search.

'As I said, I'm looking for my friend's son. Tomas. Her cousin, Lotte, gave him away when she was sent to Westerbork.'

'Yes, I know. She took him to the orphanage just outside of the Vorarlberg province, run by nuns. She told them to keep him until she could return when the war was over.'

Eva made to stand up. 'Thank you.'

Liesl held up a hand. 'There was a problem though. The Nazis were on the warpath for any Jewish children, and they tore through the towns to round them all up.'

Eva gasped. She'd heard about the children that had been sent to Auschwitz, she'd seen some of them at the camp, not many of them made it.

'They took him?' she asked, not wanting to hear it, needing to anyway.

Liesl's eyes were dark. 'The nuns were scared. Tomas had been with them for three years but they didn't want to risk his life if the Nazis found him. Lotte had told me what she'd done, in case I would need to intervene – she didn't know what would happen to her after everything that occurred at the border. She knew that I could be trusted, and take the child to a home where he could pass as a gentile. There are many families who were willing to look the other way, families who wanted a child.'

'You sent him away?'

Liesl shook her head. 'I went to fetch him last year, when they called me.'

Eva looked at her, there was a sound as the other child she'd seen walked into the house. His eyes were dark, and solemn, wary. He was dressed in thin slacks and a frayed shirt. He looked at them for a moment, his expression wary, and turned and left as quickly as he'd arrived.

Eva felt her heart began to pound. It was like staring at a ghost. Sofie was there in every single feature. Her dark eyes, the shape of her lips.

'He looks just like her,' she breathed. Tears pricked at her eyes, and her hands started to shake.

She looked at Liesl and took a deep breath. 'Thank you for looking after him. I can't tell you how grateful I am that you went to fetch him. I know it doesn't look it – from the state of me – but I will provide a good home for him, give him the love he deserves.'

Liesl stared at her in shock. Then she shook her head, her face a mixture of pity and disbelief. 'I'm sorry. I cannot just let you take *him*. I don't even know who you are!'

Eva considered the woman before her. 'No, you don't but I am not leaving Austria without him.'

Liesl stood up. 'I think you should go.'

Eva stared at the woman before her, and made no move to stand. She told herself to keep calm. A scene now would not help her. She had stared down worse, and survived. She would not leave this town without Sofie's son. 'Please, sit down. I don't mean right this minute. I'm a stranger. I can understand how you would feel that way about me – why you wouldn't want to give him to someone off the street.'

The light flaring in Liesl's eyes seemed to dissipate briefly. She nodded. 'Yes.' She studied Eva for a long moment, then reluctantly sat down. Perhaps she trusted that the strange woman in her kitchen wouldn't snatch Tomas away, not yet anyway.

'Thank you,' acknowledged Eva. 'You see, I am the boy's guardian. It was his mother's last wish that I raise him.'

Liesl shook her head, vehemently. She made a snort of disbelief. 'I don't know who you *are*, I can't just give him to you.'

Eva ran a hand through her short hair, and sighed. 'I will take that tea, if you're still offering.'

At Liesl's frown, she added, 'And I will tell you about who I am – and who Sofie was, and by the end of it, you will know what you need to do.'

# THIRTY-EIGHT

Liesl stared at her for a long moment, as if she still wanted to insist that she leave. After some time she sighed, and got up to make the tea. She could listen. If nothing else. The firm press to her lips and the stiff set of her shoulders said enough though, she wouldn't make any promises that it would change her mind.

Eva spoke for close to two hours. She described the horrors of Auschwitz, the joy of making a friend like Sofie, who had saved her life. She kept some things back, but told her everything that might help. If she was going to fight for the right to adopt her best friend's son, she would bare her soul, and she did. By the end of it, the afternoon had turned from peach to magenta, and they had drunk several cups of tea and moved on to a bottle of apple schnapps, which was the only alcohol Liesl had in her home. It was the first alcoholic drink Eva had had in years, and she sipped sparingly, even as Liesl poured herself another, tears streaming down her face. 'That poor child,' she said, meaning Sofie, swiping a hand across her nose. 'I had no idea what it was like.'

Eva nodded. No one did. What had happened was unimaginable.

'The thing is,' said Liesl, 'even if I agreed, it's Tomas. He's fragile – he's been through so much. The nuns took too long to call me, and he spent half his life learning how to hide from the Nazis. Can you imagine? He's only five years old, but if he hears the sound of boots, he runs and hides. There was no playing, no laughter. He's come a little out of his shell in the past few months – he comes out to the garden and sits near my girls, which he wouldn't do in the beginning. I don't know what another change would do to him. I haven't been able to really connect with him as much as I'd like,' she admitted.

Eva looked at her. 'Let me try. I can get to know him. Take it slowly. I can find a place nearby.'

'You'd do that?' asked Liesl.

She nodded. 'Of course.'

Liesl looked at the ground, and up at the ceiling. There were tears in her eyes. 'I've raised him as my own. I know it hasn't been long, but in my mind he is mine now, with the war being over and no one coming. I can't promise that I will be able to let him go.'

Eva looked at her. 'But you will try?'

'I can do that,' she agreed. 'If,' she stressed, 'I feel it will be better for him.'

Eva nodded. Legally she had no right to Tomas, there was no formal documentation that gave Sofie's son to her care.

She would have to convince a child who'd been scarred by the war that she should take him from the only home he'd ever known. It seemed, perhaps, an impossible task.

\*

Eva negotiated a fee with the small local hotel in exchange for some light cleaning work, helping to make the beds and clean the rooms every morning. She suspected the owner had taken pity on her more than anything. With her short hair and tiny frame, it would be some time before she didn't look like a refugee. She missed her daughter so much it felt like there was an aching wound in her chest each time she pictured her little face, so similar to her husband's.

She was grateful for the hotel's hospitality, and happy to do the work, which kept her mind occupied from all her fears and worries over how to get through to Tomas. She felt torn in two, on one hand desperate to get to know Tomas more, on the other aching to get back to her child. Sleep didn't come easily, and when it did, her dreams tormented her further.

Liesl hadn't downplayed his reticence. The first time they'd spoken hadn't gone well at all.

'Tomas?' Liesl had called, and the young child had come quickly from his small room just off the kitchen, where he'd been sitting with the small caramel-coloured dog.

'This is a friend of your mother's,' she'd said. 'She'd very much like to meet you.'

Eva stood up to greet him, and he'd taken a step back, his hands buried in the dog's wiry fur.

'Hello, Tomas,' said Eva.

He looked up at her warily, and she squatted down to his level, smiling gently. 'So you like animals, hmm?'

He nodded, and took a small step towards her. 'Your mother used to love them too. When she was a young girl, she used to keep a lot of them. Did you know that?'

He shook his head, his dark eyes wide. He looked down at the floor, then frowned. He opened and closed his mouth, then dared to ask, very quietly, 'Is – is she coming for me?'

Eva blinked, she and Liesl darted a look between them.

'No, darling,' began Eva. 'I'm sorry.'

He stared at her, then looked at the floor. 'She's dead, isn't she?'

Eva swallowed. 'Yes.'

He expelled a big breath, and Eva realised that he'd been waiting all this time for her return. Maybe in his own heart he'd clung to the hope that someday she would come get him, even though it was doubtful he remembered her at all.

'I knew it,' he said, his face turning dark and sad.

His foot kicked the side of the skirting board, and he left just as quickly as he'd arrived, the dog following closely as his heels. When they called he didn't respond, and they didn't find him for hours.

When Eva was getting ready to leave, Liesl said, 'I told you he hides. I think he thought she was going to come for him someday.'

Eva nodded, closing her eyes in pain. She straightened and then looked at Liesl who started to speak at the same time as her, 'Well, as you can—'

'I'll come back tomorrow.'

Liesl blinked, and Eva shook her head. 'I don't give up easily.'

The other woman nodded. She could see that, and respected it.

As the days passed, Eva visited Tomas every chance she got. He was quiet, shy and withdrawn. The only time she got through to him was when they took the dog for a walk by the lake. He liked the water, and kept trying to skim rocks against the surface. 'Let me show you,' said Eva, picking up a flat rock, and shaking it in her hand, till it went bounding against the lake making several dips before it finally sunk some distance away.

'How did you do that?' he said in surprise, and she was able for a moment to see the child beneath the solemn mask.

'It's all about the wrist,' she said, teaching him how to throw it.

'Did my mother show you that?' he asked. It was one of the first times he'd asked her a question about her.

Eva shook her head. 'My uncle Bedrich,' she responded. As she said his name aloud, his beloved craggy face peered in her mind's eye, doffing his grey hat at her, before he left with a wink. She felt tears prickle her eyes: what had happened to him? Was he alive? Were her parents? She had to draw in a deep breath as Tomas peered up at her waiting, shaking off the dark pull of her thoughts. 'We have a summer house, it's also near a lake – much smaller than this one, but it's private, amongst the mountains. There are otters,' she said with a smile. 'I learnt to skim rocks there.'

Her heart burst when he gave her a tentative smile in return.

Once they headed back to the house, after their walks he would become quiet again, not saying much.

'I'll see you tomorrow, Tomas,' she said, before he disappeared.

He turned back to look at her, nodded once, then left.

As the weeks passed, Tomas opened up to her more. He wanted to know about Sofie and she was happy to tell him. He liked to hear about Naděje too. 'She's broken?' he said, when she'd tried to explain about her weak state.

'She's fragile,' said Eva. 'She's been through a lot. If you meet her you'll have to be gentle.'

'I can do that,' he said with a solemn look. Then he admitted, 'I feel broken sometimes too.'

Eva had to breathe deeply to keep herself from crying. She nodded, 'Me too.'

The day he let her take his hand, she knew he was ready. 'Tomas, I'd like you to come to live with me. It's what your mother wanted,' she swallowed. 'I'd like it very much – but if you want to stay here I will understand.'

If that's what he wanted, it would be the hardest thing she'd ever have to accept, but she would do it. As much as she'd promised Sofie – as much as she'd fallen for this little boy, with his serious eyes, and his quiet smile – she couldn't make his life harder, she could understand what Liesl had meant, now. How no matter what they all thought, what they all wanted, his needs had to come first.

To her surprise, he touched her hand. 'Aunt Liesl asked me if that's what I'd like, and I said yes – I would like to be with you. I'd like to meet Naděje, and live by that lake, to hear more stories about my mother.'

She clutched him to her tightly, and cried into his dark blond hair. 'I will tell you all the stories you want to know, we will be a family, all of us,' she promised him.

He looked up at her with his dark eyes, and smiled, her heart felt like it would burst when his little arms tightened around her in response.

# THIRTY-NINE

Eva returned to *Jívka* in the autumn, and together with Tomas, Naděje, Kaja and Helga began a new life in the countryside. It was wondrous to have her baby girl back in her arms, and her heart tore at how much she'd grown in the short space she'd been away. It wasn't much; she was still a tiny little thing, and would likely remain so for most of her life, but it hurt to know she'd missed it. It was worth it though to have Tomas in her life. As the weeks had passed he had begun slowly to open up more, and it was clear that from the moment he'd clamped eyes on Naděje he was in her thrall.

He was a beautiful child, with his mother's eyes. More at home in the outdoors, befriending the wildlife, than he'd ever been cooped up for so long in a cloister. Liesl had allowed the boy to take the small caramel-coloured dog, whose name was Duster, with him, which Eva was grateful for – as at least he would have some normalcy when starting his new life with her. She taught him how to sketch, and the three of them would spend hours exploring the lake, Naděje asleep in her pram, while she and Tomas sought the dens of otters, and convinced a stray cat to make theirs his home of choice. It broke her heart to think of the five years Sofie had missed – but every time he looked at her, something like a wry smile on his lips, she couldn't help but see her face.

\*

While her days were full of a lightness she'd been hard pressed to imagine discovering, at night, her dreams took her back to the darkness, and she woke, shivering and full of fear, tears coursing down her cheeks.

When Helga heard her one night, she came to lie next to her, fitting her body next to hers the way they'd all lain in their bunks. 'It's all right, you're safe now,' she said.

Eva nodded. She looked up at the old woman, and squeezed her hand. 'Do you remember when we first met?'

Helga sighed. 'I wasn't nice, I'm sorry.'

On her first night in Auschwitz, Helga had told her that they were all going to die – she accused her of being a fool because she vowed that she was going to live, that she would see Michal again someday. Eva couldn't help marvelling at how the woman who'd been so close to giving up on living when they'd met was a different person all round.

'You told me I was a fool to hope.'

'I was wrong.'

Eva brushed away her tears. 'Maybe, maybe not. I really believed that we'd get out of it together, Sofie and me. That I would find Michal.'

'But you did – you proved me so wrong, *dítě*.'

Eva wasn't so sure sometimes. With no word from her parents or her uncle, she was beginning to face the fact that maybe she was the only one left.

'I think you should speak to someone about these nightmares,' Helga said. 'It's good to get it out.'

'I don't know if I could sit and tell someone about this – I told Liesl and that was one of the hardest things to do – and I barely scratched the surface. The only person I want to tell is Michal, and I can't.'

Helga nodded. 'You could write to him. I do that in my notebook. I write to my husband, my children. I tell him how I feel, what I'm going through, it helps. Especially with the nightmares.'

Eva thought about it, and she nodded. Already she'd disturbed Tomas with hers – she didn't want him to fear for her, didn't want him to grow up with any more darkness than he'd already faced.

The next morning while Tomas played outside in the late autumn sunshine with the cat, and Naděje slept in her cot, Eva wrote letters. To Michal. To her mother, her father, Sofie, Mila, and her uncle Bedrich. All the things she needed to tell them, all the last words she'd wished she could have told them. She cried as the words began to pour out, needing to be said. She told Sofie how she was sorry, how she wished things had worked out differently. She told her uncle how grateful she

277

was for the lessons he'd given her. But most of all she spoke to Michal.

*My darling,*

*My deepest regret is that you never got to meet your daughter. She is a miracle that happened to us in that horrific place. So small, so full of spirit, so full of life. I look at her, and draw strength, and remember that I can keep going.*

*I look at her, and I see you. She looks so much like you, Michal, and it breaks my heart in two as much as it melts it. I swear I saw a dimple in her cheek the other day, just like yours. I had to go for a walk by myself, and try to stop the tears. Not let poor Tomas see, he doesn't need tears now, just hugs and laughter and that's what I'm trying to give that dear child. You'd love him so much if you knew him too.*

*My darling, I told Helga that hope had kept me alive. But it was love. My love for you, and it helped me so much more than anything else did, it brought our child into the world and helped me find Tomas. When they all thought I was a fool, all I could think of was seeing you again.*

*I thank you for that, for the beautiful love we shared, it saved my life.*

As the days passed she wrote two dozen letters, and in the last one, she told him how she was going to try to live. *I made a promise to my friend, and I am going to honour it. She died for our daughter so that we could live. I owe her that. I will always love you.* She placed the letters in her drawer, and someday she would give them to Naděje, so that she could know their story. For now, she would give her the things she would give Tomas, love, and laughter, and a home, safe from darkness.

As autumn gave its final burst, and the leaves around the lake turned to copper and russet, Eva watched as Tomas ran towards the lake, Duster at his heels, the last of the autumn sunshine turning the lake into shimmering gold, then suddenly stopped, and frowned, pointing up ahead, and said, 'Man?'

Eva stopped, and looked. Shading her eyes against the afternoon sun, she saw the colour gold, and then a man in the distance. He was walking painstakingly, slowly.

She blinked, and stood stock still, not able to move.

Something about him looked familiar, but she couldn't, wouldn't trust her brain.

'It's not,' she breathed.

As he neared, he looked up, then he stopped as well.

There was a shout from the house, and Kaja's voice called out, 'Michal?'

Eva put both hands across her mouth, and then began to walk, slowly, then very fast, towards the figure at the end of the drive. He started to walk towards her as quickly as his legs would allow.

She didn't pause to see his face – suddenly, his arm was around her, and she sunk into the familiar embrace. She couldn't stop the tears, even as he kissed her face, her hair, her hands. Even as Tomas rushed forward to meet this stranger.

'B-but how?' stuttered Eva, not able to let him go. Not sure if her broken heart had made him appear, if she hadn't slipped into a delusion of some kind. Part of her didn't care even if that was the case.

His face was worn, and he looked years older than he should have. There was grey streaked through his hair. Dark shadows beneath his eyes, which were heavily lined. His frame was thin, and his left hand hung limply at his side, she could see a heavy knot of scars, and two fingers missing. She held it gently.

'I wrote you letters but I don't think you got them,' he said, touching her face, her short hair which had begun at last to grow around her ears. 'I found out later why – when I saw what was left of the apartment. It took such a long time to cross the border. My birth certificate is German, even though my family lived here most of my life, they didn't want to let me in. The Americans and the Red Cross helped me – I convinced them to let me come home.'

Eva's lips trembled as she listened to his voice, as she stared up at his face, her eyes filled.

'B-but they said you were dead – an accident at the factory.'

He shook his head. 'I got these injuries,' he said, holding up his hand, his face a little sad. 'I don't know if I'll be able to play again,' he said, then shrugged. 'Someone else died, his tattoo was the same as mine, except for the nine. We were friends.' He breathed out now as he realised. 'All this time, I never realised they would have recorded it as me.'

Eva gasped. He'd been alive, this whole time?

He held her fiercely. 'Oh God, Eva, I dreamt of this for so long,' he said, kissing her, holding her close.

'Me too,' she said, softly, and started to cry again. She touched his face. In the background she could see Tomas staring at them, waiting to come forward, his curiosity running rampant. She smiled, and beckoned him over, as Helga came forward too, their small daughter in her arms. She led her husband towards them. 'There's someone I think you might like to meet.'

# FORTY

*Prague, Present day*

Naděje sat at her desk, overlooking the city of Prague, which the dawn light had bathed the colour of gold. The colour of love, of champagne and her mother's laugh. Thinking of her life, of her parents, and the enduring love they had shared.

Her granddaughter, Kamila, had come to check in on her, and she paused her story for a moment, her pen poised over the sheet of paper, inviting her to take a seat.

'I moved back here just after the end of Communist rule,' she said. 'I wanted to know where I came from. But really,' she said, looking down at her stacks of paper, scribbled in her messy handwriting, from the tale she'd put off for all these years which had finally been set down, transcribed from her mother's letters, her legacy to her, 'I was born in Auschwitz.'

Kamila nodded. She knew a little of the story, but not everything.

'My mother was a remarkable woman, and she taught me about love. She was patient, and kind. As you know, it took me years before I was able to walk. She tried her best to undo what had been done to me through their mistreatment of her, but it is a legacy I have lived with all my life. I have broken countless bones in my life, and suffered from a weak chest. At five feet, I am often the smallest person in the room.'

'No, you're not,' said Kamila, shaking her head, and her grandmother looked at her, a frown between her eyes.

'You're the most compelling, sometimes the most infuriating person because you are always right – you always know just what to say to win every argument, here and in your lectures at the university. What you lack in size is often overlooked by the force of your personality.'

'Are you trying to say that I am stubborn? Or a hard-arse?' asked Naděje, with a quirk to her lips.

Kamila laughed at the American term. 'Both. It's the other thing you got from them maybe.'

Naděje smiled. 'Yes. Stubborn love, that's what my mother called it.'

Stubborn love, that was the legacy of her life growing up. After the Communists took over, her father got a job offer in England, and they decided to move, and they took to their new lives with the same gutsy determination that had led them back to one another.

In their home in the countryside, her parents raised her and her brother Tomas, who remained Naděje's best friend throughout their lives. As far as both of them knew their grandmother was a stern-looking woman named Helga – it would be years before Naděje discovered that they weren't, in fact, related. It didn't matter. 'Sometimes you get to choose your family,' was another thing her mother used to like to say.

Discovering what had happened to her parents, and her beloved uncle Bedrich, through a chance meeting with one of their old neighbours, had been devastating for her mother. Eva's father had died in transit to Auschwitz from typhus, and her mother and uncle had been gassed in the Terezín family camp in Auschwitz: they had been there a few short weeks while Eva had been there too, and no one had ever known. This fact would haunt her for years. Like the nightmares that never really left her. They were indelible scars.

'Despite all this, my parents had an unconquerable lust for life, and together they fought hard against the darkness,' she wrote, continuing her story as Kamila got up to open the curtains.

'My mother found it hard to draw at first, but in time she began to paint again, and she sold a few. My father taught music at a local school, and he always composed new pieces that reminded him of his sweetheart, and his children. Every Friday, without fail, my mother made *challah* bread and lit a candle for the woman who had saved them, her best friend Sofie.'

Then she wrote the final words of their story. 'I was never meant to live, but I have, because of her. Because of them, and despite all the horror in this world, all its darkness that tried so desperately to wipe us out, my life has been one full of joy, light, and love because no matter how hard someone tries to vanquish the day, what I have learnt in my long years in this life, is that dawn breaks even the longest night.'

# A LETTER FROM LILY

Vera Bein gave birth to her daughter, Angela Orosz, in the top bunk of camp C at Auschwitz-Birkenau in December 1944. She weighed just 1kg and was too weak to cry. It is what saved her.

The result of malnutrition, and the harsh conditions of the camp, as well as an experimentation on her pregnant mother by the famous Nazi doctor, Dr Josef Mengele, ensured that the effects of the camp stayed with her for her entire life. She didn't walk during her early years, and suffered many adverse health effects such as brittle bones and weak lungs. Her mother had arrived at the camp three months pregnant and was forced to undergo experiments from Mengele, but managed to slip through his clutches and survive. She got assigned a job in the kitchen, and when she gave birth, the *Blockalteste* made her climb to the top bunk and helped her give birth.

Her remarkable true story and others' inspired this novel.

I also drew on the true stories of survivors like Eva Schloss, the step-sister of Anne Frank, who survived Auschwitz, along with her mother, by staying behind with the sick and elderly when they were ordered to join the death marches, a decision that ultimately saved their lives.

I got a sense of life in Prague and the ghetto of Terezín from Helga Weiss, who kept a diary, as well as drawing poignant sketches of her time in a concentration camp. Helga, like the others, also survived Auschwitz. I was also greatly inspired by the incredibly poignant story of Anka Bergman, who also came to Auschwitz pregnant, and had her baby on the train on the way to the Mauthausen death camp. The only reason she survived was because the day before the Nazis had blown up the crematoria.

It has been an honour and a privilege to share some of these remarkable women's experiences in my novel. After months of getting to know these women through their written testimonies and biographies, I noticed one thing that each one of them shared – an unquenchable sense of hope that they would survive. In fact, throughout each woman's story, they made a point of saying that they were likely being foolish. I felt that this was significant, somehow. While of course they had no real control over their fates within the camp, it is incredible that they held onto this sense of hope despite the darkness they encountered, and I feel that perhaps in some small way it did end up making a difference to their survival – perhaps in helping them see a way out. It is hard to say. So much of survival depended on luck and timing.

In the early period of the existence of the women's camp, babies born there were put to death, regardless of their ethnicity, without being entered in the camp records.

Babies born to Jewish mothers in Auschwitz were put to death until November 1944, when the mass extermination of the Jews came to a halt.

Records show that at least seven hundred children were born in Auschwitz-Birkenau. To date only a handful are known to have survived.

LilyRoseGrahamAuthor

@lilygrahambooks

www.lilygraham.net

# ACKNOWLEDGEMENTS

I couldn't have written this novel without the guiding hand of my incredible editor, Lydia Vassar-Smith. Thank you so much for all that you've done in bringing this story to life, pointing me in the right direction, and always with such a kind heart. I am so incredibly fortunate to work with you.

I never meant to write a story about Auschwitz. I'd been trying desperately to make headway with the other novel I was *meant* to write, and encountered writer's block for the first time, when I came across the story of a woman whose mother had been told she would never fall pregnant after being in a concentration camp. The idea of a child born out of such darkness caught hold of me and just would not let go, and every time I tried to write that other book, the words refused to come. I looked up other survivor stories, and then read biographies, and before I knew it, I realised this was the story I needed to write – and so had to write my editor a letter to that effect. Incredibly, she said yes. The only trouble was now I had to write a story that tested me beyond anything else I'd ever done before. She held my hand, even as I doubted myself and patiently coaxed me through the other side, step by step. My husband did the same.

I never meant to write this story, but I feel incredibly honoured to have done so, so that others like me may know more about the remarkable women who experienced one of the most horrific periods in history, and survived. I can only hope that you will forgive any inaccuracies that may have occurred in the process.

My deepest, heartfelt thanks to the team at Bookouture for their enormous support over the years. It takes a village to bring a book out to the world, but only one person's name gets to be on the cover. Thank you so much to the amazing team who have helped and supported me, fixed my grammar, designed the beautiful covers, and generally made me very proud to work with them.

Thank you to my friends and family for always being there with a supportive ear and a kind word.

Last and especially not least, thank you to you, the readers and bloggers who have shared your support and kindness for my writing over the years – I couldn't have done this without you. Thank you to all my wonderful readers who have sent me tweets and checked in on me making sure I was still alive while I was AWOL from social media, writing this novel, such as the marvellous Kathy Schaffer. I am blessed to have your support.